CHILKOOT CHALLENGE

by

ANNE INNIS DAGG

Chilkoot Challenge

Copyright © 2020 by Anne Innis Dagg

All rights reserved

Published by Otter Press

First edition

This book is a work of fiction. Names, characters, places and incidents either are products of the author's imagination or are used fictitiously.

No part of this book may be reproduced, or stored in a retrieval system, or transmitted in any form or by any means, electronic, mechanical, photocopying, recording, or otherwise, without express written permission of the publisher.

Cover photo: Anne Innis Dagg

ISBN 979857806586

In the 1980s, with my children old enough to look after themselves or at summer camps, I spent months in the wilderness of northern Canada, travelling by canoe with groups containing an assortment of people, including my husband, women friends, and students. Perhaps I wanted to emulate my father with his love of the north? Certainly I wanted to see as many wild animals as possible. At a Writers' Union Conference I spoke to Pierre Berton about my idea to paddle the Yukon River. He told me how to go about planning the trip, including where to rent a canoe; he had recently completed the trip himself with his family, as reported in his book *Drifting Home*.

This story was inspired by my memorable Yukon trip with five other women, including my sister-in-law Wendy Innis, in 1985. Although I have written many non-fiction books, this is my one and only fictional endeavour.

CHILKOOT
CHALLENGE

Chapter 1

"Look, it's a bald eagle, my first bald eagle!" Alice shouted. She leapt up from where she had been sorting out bits and pieces--matches for the hike in one pile, bailing sponge for the canoe in a second--and sprinted for one of the windows at the edge of the deck. Beyond the ship, less than fifty yards away, a fir tree glided slowly past, the magnificent eagle perched serenely on its top branch.

"He isn't bald at all," she whooped. "Those are white feathers on his head. Look at that beak!" The bird remained in profile, glaring south at the narrow waterway through which they had come. Pat and May were now beside Alice, peering at the small dot of white slowly receding behind them, the brown body already indistinguishable from the dark foliage.

"I should get my camera out, mére," Alice said to May, her mother. "Where did I put it?" She wanted to illustrate the journal she was keeping.

"In the duffel," May said.

The three of them moved back to the small space they had cleared among the deck chairs to continue sorting out their belongings. Most of their camping gear would go with them on their four-day hike over the Chilkoot trail. The rest, which they would need only on the river, would be shipped by a friend by bus from Skagway to meet them in Whitehorse after they had finished the hike.

Alice plunged into the duffel bag, pulling out a tarpaulin, whistle, flashlight, lipstick, a frying pan, socks, and a bag of brown rice. She dropped them in a heap on the deck.

"Here it is," she said, finding at last her Instamatic. "I'm just going to see if they're any more eagles. He was gorgeous!"

"He or she," Pat corrected. "Both sexes look the same."

"Whatever," said Alice, fiddling with her lens as she edged away.

"What about this mess?" asked her mother, looking at their belongings strewn about.

"I'll be right back," Alice promised. She trotted to the companionway at the edge of the ship leading to the deck below.

May sighed as she and Pat went back to sorting. "I hope it works out, having Alice along," she said. "She was desperate to come and she's as strong as we are, maybe stronger."

"That's not saying much," Pat laughed, "but she'll be fine. She's mature in a way for sixteen, and enthusiastic as well. I like the way she treats your friends as her friends."

"She feels you are her friends, even if you are older. She's been around adults all her life, even before her father left us."

Pat began to shake out the blue tent which had been folded too loosely to fit into her backpack.

"Alice was telling me about a competition you're entering. What's it about? Why didn't you tell Fay and me?"

The two women crouched opposite each other, smoothing and straightening the tent which lay in disarray between them, rolling it up bit by bit. May worked away without looking at Pat.

"I didn't think you'd be interested," she said. "You're not into photography. Here, kneel on this end." Pat and May were similar in age, but very different in style. May looked every inch the professional in her tailored blouse and slacks, while Pat looked almost frumpy in faded jeans and billowing shirt.

"Still, I would have thought you would mention it. Two thousand dollars is a lot of money. What exactly do you have to do? This tent will never fit!" She gave the tent a mighty shake, then began to roll it up all over again, pulling the plastic floor tight with each twist of her hands. She shoved the mosquito netting of the door and window among the folds of the material.

"Alaska and the Yukon are sponsoring the contest. I read about it in a photography magazine I ordered for the college library. They want a tourist package, that's what they called it, a 'Tourist Package' that they can use for publicity to lure tourists to the north-west. It has to be about the Goldrush Trail of 1898 that men used to get to Dawson City. The tent will surely fit now."

May held the case so that Pat could stuff the bundle of tent into it. Then she pulled the drawstring of the case and tied it securely.

"Women too," added Pat, who taught women's studies at the same college in Edmonton as May. She leant down to push the tent under a chair, then stopped.

"That's why you organized our trip to hike up the Chilkoot Trail and then come down the Yukon River," Pat exclaimed, suddenly clear as to why May had been so set on this one route for their summer adventure.

"It's a terrific route even if there weren't a prize," May said defensively. "Let's not talk too loudly though – the less competition the better." She looked around at a bearded man who was dozing on his deck chair and at a woman who sat cross-legged on the deck strumming on a guitar while singing softly to herself. Neither was paying any attention to them.

"Can anyone enter?" Pat asked. Before they could answer, Fay appeared, hurrying toward them from the front of the ship. "We're coming to whales soon," she said in excitement. "The Forest Ranger announced it to the people in the front lounge." Fay wore blue slacks and a pink ruffled blouse under her pale blue sweater.

"Do you know about the $2,000 Tourist Package contest?" Pat asked Fay, ignoring May, who was frowning at her.

"What's that?" said Fay. She turned to Pat and gave her a big smile, she was so pleased to be on holiday. A secretary at the Edmonton College, she was much younger at thirty than the other two, and even more poorly paid. She had met the others at a Keep-Fit class.

"Alaska and Yukon are offering a $2,000 prize to the person who can come up with the best publicity for the Skagway to Dawson City route that we're taking," Pat said. "May's going to take photos for it as we go along."

"That's wonderful," Fay said to May. "Can anyone enter?"

"I guess so," said May. "Did you see Alice?" May always brought in her daughter when she wanted to change the subject.

"Yes," said Fay. "She's talking to a handsome hunk on the deck below."

"Does it have to be photos?" Fay asked May.

"The ad about it was in a photography magazine," May answered. "but it only talked about as a Tourist Package," she added slowly. "There's less than a month left before the entries have to be in at Dawson City. They'll decide the winner at the Discovery Day celebration in mid-August."

"That's when we will be in Dawson City," said Pat. "What fun!"

"Yes," May agreed. "Here's Alice again."

Alice came bounding along the deck, her long brown hair flying around her. As she came in out of the wind, she pushed it back from her face.

"Can I have the binocs, Mom? We're coming to humpback country in about half an hour. The Forest Ranger is going to talk about what we see in the lounge. She has some neat pamphlets for my journal."

"They're in my pack under my chair, in the pocket on the left," May said.

Alice got down on her knees to pull out her mother's pack. There were about fifty deck chairs spread out on the covered deck, each claimed by someone with a packsack underneath or a sleeping bag on top, but the atmosphere was so relaxed that no one seemed to worry that their gear might be stolen. Each Alaskan ferry sailing from Prince Rupert to Skagway operated more like a bus than a stately ship, stopping frequently at small ports so that people and vehicles could get on and off. The cars and campers had to make reservations months in advance, but those on foot came and went as the spirit moved them. The four women, who had taken the train from Edmonton to Prince Rupert, loved the informality of the ferry.

"What were you talking about?" Alice asked as she pulled out the field glasses, scattering bottles of mosquito repellent and water disinfectant pills on the deck around her. She was conscious that a silence had fallen when she joined the others.

"About the Tourist Package contest," Fay said slowly. "Do you know about it?"

"Of course. That's why we're here, isn't it?" Pat and Fay looked at each other in slight surprise. "Mére's going to win $2,000," she grinned at them. "Or maybe I will. I may write a poem about the Goldrush Trail. I'm rather good at rhyming. Some of my journal is in poetry."

"Now Alice, don't be silly," May said. "Where will you be with the field glasses? I'll come in a moment and join you."

"On the deck below this." Alice wrestled the backpack under the chair, jumped to her feet and ran off.

"She's just fooling," May said. "I am sure a poem would not do at all. The judges will be looking for a series of first-rate pictures, and that's my profession, taking pictures. Come on, it's time for whales." She threaded her way among the deck chairs to follow her daughter.

"Funny she never told us about the contest, though," said Pat to Fay.

"Really funny," Fay agreed wryly.

Chapter 2

The whale watching was a great success! It was raining slightly, so most of the passengers crowded into the lounge where the Forest Ranger gave a running commentary on the various flippers and flukes which appeared without warning on the grey water around them.

"Look, over by the shore, two flukes!" Alice called to the others.

"That'll be humpback whales," commented the Forest Ranger into her microphone. "You can tell them because they're the biggest, the biggest whales in Frederick Sound, up to thirty-five feet long. They're on the port opposite the ship."

After some confusion about what "port" meant, the passengers crowded to the left side to see the mother and young apparently feeding in shallow water.

"There's a blow between them and us!" Alice now exclaimed after searching the surface of the water with the field glasses.

"Where? Where?" an old man asked beside her.

"There," Alice pointed in excitement to a cloud of steam rising just above the water, "about one hundred metres away."

"Come now, you and your metric," he said, turning away without another glance over the water.

"Here's a fin on the right," a boy shouted.

"A fin to starboard," announced the Ranger, officially, and the watchers streamed to the other side of the ship to try to spot this new diversion. "It could be a killer whale."

"Ç'est comme une danse," a young woman from Québec said to her husband. They couldn't understand what the Ranger was saying, but her announcements were followed by the swarm of listeners jockeying for position at some new spot at the edge of the lounge.

"Pas si gracieuse, peut-être," the husband laughed, as youngsters pushed their way in front of the taller adults.

"You have the eyes of an eagle," Alice heard a voice at her shoulder.

She turned to see Mike, the young man she had met earlier who was also bound for the Chilkoot trail.

"I'm not bald, though," she laughed.

"Thank goodness no," he said, eying her shiny hair.

"Are you going further north than Whitehorse?" Alice asked him, now finding the bits of whale she was glimpsing rather a bore.

"To Dawson City," Mike replied.

"So are we," Alice enthused. "My mom and two of her friends from the college where she teaches."

"I'm with my friend Tim," Mike said. "I guess you're renting canoes in Whitehorse too."

Alice nodded. Mike looked pretty old to her, perhaps twenty-five or so, but he seemed nice enough.

"Here's Tim now," said Mike, as his friend strolled toward them swinging both field glasses and an expensive camera in his hand.

"And here's my friend Fay," Alice said, as Fay came up, attracted by the young men.

The four adventurers introduced themselves to each other, then began to discuss their plans.

"We've planned on four days for the Chilkoot, a day or two in Whitehorse to buy supplies, then two weeks on the Yukon. We have to be in Dawson City by mid-August to do some legal work before the tourist season closes," said Tim.

"You're lawyers, are you?" asked Fay brightly.

"Almost. We both have to finish articling, but that should be done before Christmas. We work for Mike's dad's law firm, which is how we got this trip organized."

"You're lucky," said Alice.

"Lucky to get the time off, but unlucky because it's not paid, not even our Dawson City work."

"Don't tell me you're after the $2,000, too?" laughed Fay. "Every other person and their dog is."

"What $2,000?" Mike and Tim asked, almost together.

May perhaps heard the chorus, because just then she called from across the lounge. "Alice, Fay, hurry, there's a huge whale here, right beside the ship!"

The four of them rushed to join her, along with the most enduring of the other passengers.

"Where--Where--Where?" asked Alice.

"Right here--maybe it'll come up again," May's voice was full of excitement.

"I didn't see anything, and I've been sitting here for ages," the man beside her said.

"Just a glimpse of black fin, maybe a killer whale," May went on, ignoring him.

They all stared out at the water beside and behind the ship, but there was no further sign of whales.

"Oh well, maybe next time," May said finally.

"Come on now, Fay and Alice, we must go up and finish repacking." She bustled toward the door so quickly, turning to wait for the others to follow her, that they had no chance to introduce her to Tim and Mike.

"We'll see you later," said Fay.

"You bet," said Tim. The two men continued to stare at the water, but they saw no more flukes or fins.

After dinner, when the women were sitting in the cafeteria with their coffee, Alice brought up the subject of the two men.

"They're going on the same route as us, so we could join forces with them," Alice suggested. "Mére said there was safety in numbers, in case one of us breaks a leg or is eaten by a bear."

"Don't be silly," May countered. "I only said that when we were considering going by ourselves, before Pat and Fay agreed to come too. Now there are four of us, we'll be fine."

"I agree with Alice," said Fay. "They're both nice, lawyers, and it would be fun to go in a bunch."

"What are you saying," said Pat angrily. "The four of us arranged to go together. The last thing we need are a couple of men hanging around. Men may have their place, but it's not on our holiday."

"It was just an idea," said Fay. "There's no need to get your tail in a knot."

"If they came along it would look as if a bunch of women couldn't manage on their own."

"Okay, okay, have it your own way," said Fay crossly. "You always do anyway, but I don 't know why you hate men so much. They're just people, after all."

Alice did not like to see the two friends argue. "Why don't we keep separate from them except when it will save us money." This seemed to her like a sensible compromise.

"I thought you said they were lawyers," May asked Fay sharply. "Lawyers don't need to worry about money."

"Well, apprentice lawyers, actually. They're still articling."

"Tomorrow we have to take a taxi from the dock to Dyea, the start of the Chilkoot," Alice continued. "Mére said I was to look after finances, since I'm a whiz at arithmetic," she smiled modestly. "We could save money if we used two taxis for the six of us. Otherwise we'll have to take two for ourselves, since we couldn't get all four of us and our gear in one."

"It's only ten miles to Dyea," said May. "That won't be much."

"But you said we shouldn't waste money," Alice said puzzled.

"I think Pat's right. We don't want to be dependent on other people."

"You don 't seem to like Tim and Mike, yet you haven 't even met them," Fay said to May and Pat.

"I'm sure they're fine men, but I think it's hard enough to get along well with a group of people you know. It seems to me to be courting danger to add more people you know nothing about," said Pat.

While the women argued, Tim and Mike were laying out their sleeping bags on the lounge chairs set out in rows on the middle deck.

"I'm going to turn in early," said Mike. "Tomorrow's the first day of the hike."

"Me too," said Tim.

They lay side by side, staring at the ceiling, too relaxed to climb into their sleeping bags to begin the night in earnest.

"I'd stay away from Alice, if I were you. She's just a kid," Tim said suddenly.

"I know that. I'm not into robbing cradles. She's a nice kid though, full of beans."

They lay silent for a while as other indoor types slowly joined them, choosing lounge chairs near or far from the lights, near or far from the door, near or far from the aisle where people would be passing back and forth during the night as new passengers joined the Malaspina and old ones departed.

"What about Fay?" asked Mike. "Is she your type?"

"A little old, but not bad. Friendly."

"Let's stay clear of that group if we can. What we don't need is a bunch of women cluttering up our trip. Especially those two old ones."

"I wonder what they meant about $2,000. I could really use that kind of money right now."

"You're not kidding. I'll ask Alice in the morning."

"Good night then. I'm turning in."

"Good night."

Slowly silence fell over the sleeping men in the indoor lounge, and over Alice and her friends on the deck above, lying quietly side by side on four deck chairs. Alice snuggled into her sleeping bag contentedly, her face pressed against the plastic strips of her chair. Tomorrow their adventure would really begin. She fell asleep as she planned what she would put in her journal in the morning.

Chapter 3

Everyone was excited the next day as the Malaspina left the dock at Haines and turned along the Lynn Canal toward Skagway. It was a fine day, brisk, with only a few white clouds in the blue sky. The passengers watched with awe as steep mountain slopes passed by on either side. The four adventurers stood by the railing, gazing happily about.

Soon they saw Skagway, nestled at the foot of the mountains ahead of them. Its buildings were several stories high, one with bulb-shaped towers, but they looked tiny against the backdrop.

A loud speaker voice announced that drivers should go to their cars, ready to debark after the ship docked. Shortly after, the pedestrians, too, were directed to D dock.

"Isn't this exciting?" May asked her daughter, squeezing her arm. They had spent part of the morning finishing their packing, and were now ready to begin the hike. The four adventurers shuffled forward together among the "walk-ons," each looking overloaded, their large backpacks hung about with necessities such as rolled-up air-bubble mattress, water bottle, sleeping bag, tent, and hiking boots.

"I don't think I'm over thirty pounds," Fay commented, "but this pack is sure going to feel heavy at the end of a day."

"I left out absolutely everything I won't need. Even my deodorant," Pat said. "I hope I'm not too high when we get to Whitehorse."

"I hope so too," laughed Alice.

"Don 't you have any hiking boots?" May asked Fay who was wearing Oxfords with rubber soles.

"I couldn't afford them. These should be okay. They have a good grip."

The large door at the front of the ship slowly lowered after a slight bump had signalled their arrival at Skagway. It formed a ramp over which the cars and people immediately began to stream.   The pedestrians were directed through a small building with a waiting room and lockers. Beyond it a row of taxis waited to drive fares to the town a fair distance away. Many of the hikers set off on foot, but others crowded into the taxis. There was only one left when the four women arrived in front of the building.

"We need two taxis," said Pat. "What shall we do?"

"We can let Mike and Tim have it," Fay said, noticing just then that the two men, as loaded-down with gear as they were, were next in line behind them.   None of the women had seen them since the day before.

Before anyone could say anything, she called to them "You take this taxi. We need two, so we can get the next two that come."

"Thanks, Fay," said Tim. "That's good of you."

The two of them lowered their backpacks carefully off their backs, lifted them into the open trunk of the taxi, closed it, and climbed into the back seat. The taxi rushed off across the large parking lot with a squeal of tires.

May glared at Fay. "What did you do that for? I thought we arranged to keep clear of them."

"That was your idea, not mine," Fay snapped. "I believe in being friendly even if you don't."

"We could have used that taxi to take our duffels to the bus station. That'll take some time. Then we could have met with the second taxi at Dyea."

"Oh well, we 're not in any huge rush," soothed Pat. "We have four whole days to relax in without worrying about time."

"I don't know if relax is what we'll be doing, if your pack feels as heavy as mine," Alice laughed.

"It's probably better if we don't part ranks anyway," Pat continued. "We don't want to take a chance on missing each other."

"You should take a picture of Skagway from here," Alice said to her mother. She wanted to take her mind off the taxi that had just escaped.

"All right," May said. She took out her camera while Fay walked moodily to the edge of the water beside the building. Pat followed her.

"Never mind, May," she said to Fay. "She's just on edge because she wants the trip to go well. She feels responsible because she organized it."

"She's so bossy. I think she wants to keep everyone else from trying for the $2,000, that's what I think. She has more money than I have, so why does she have to be so selfish?"

"She prides herself on being a professional photographer, I guess," said Pat.

"Real professionals don't mind competition."

It took fifteen minutes for the next taxi to arrive, but fortunately, it was followed closely by a second. Alice and her mother got into the first, and

Pat and Fay into the second. They drove together to the bus station, which turned out to be a desk in the lobby of a hotel, and then to Dyea, a bay just north of Skagway. Here Alice paid the two taxis, noting the amount in the account book her mother had given her for the trip, while the others unloaded the packs.

"Here we are, gang. We're off to make our fortunes," called Pat. She put her foot on her backpack as if it were a newly-killed lion.

"Gold, gold, marvellous gold!" shouted Alice, joining her.

"Let me snap the three of you," said Fay, who had a Brownie of utmost simplicity. She had always wanted to be an artist and liked to draw sketches from photographs when she had the time.

"Smile everybody," said May, reflecting Fay's good mood. "This may be the last time we'll feel like it until we reach Dawson City!" The three of them grinned like crazy, their arms draped over each other's shoulders, while May photographed them.

While May fiddled with the shoulder straps of her backpack, the others drifted to a notice board and to a visitor book where Alice entered their names.

"It says here black bears are more common before the summit and grizzlies after, when we get back into Canada," Pat said.

"And here it says keep warm and dry, to prevent hypothermia," said Pat. "Whatever that is."

"And here it says no artifacts, nothing left by human beings in the past, can be removed from the trail," said Fay. "I thought there were only boilers and stoves left; it would be hard to lug them out."

"How about first camp at Canyon City? That's eight miles from here. Okay?" May was ready to start off at last, followed by the others who quickly donned their packs.

"Okay"

"Okay"

"Aye aye, sir"

The first mile was hard, up and down the twisting path through a dense, hilly forest, but after that the going became easier as the trail followed an old logging track. The hikers might have felt relieved at this change for the better, but they didn't. Their packs were already beginning to be foremost in their consciousness. For shoulders and backs unaccustomed to carrying anything more than clothing, even thirty pounds can soon begin to seem like fifty or seventy. At first, Alice had been delighted with how light her backpack had felt. She knew how heavy ten pounds of potatoes were when she carried them from their car up the stairs to their apartment on shopping days, and now her load didn't even seem that bad, what with the padded shoulder and waist straps. Later, she was amazed at how painful her muscles were. She clasped her hands behind her back for awhile to relieve her aching shoulders, then tried hooking her hands into the shoulder straps to stop them from cutting into her. Nothing staved off the discomfort for long.

"Let's rest for a minute," she said at last. "This is Finnegan 's Point—see, there's the sign."

"Good idea," said Fay. "My back is killing me."

"Even my feet ache," groaned Pat.

May felt as desperate as the others but didn't say anything. If the leader complains, where will it all end? she thought. Perhaps all heading back for Skagway and the bus for Whitehorse! She had to smile at the thought.

"This is where people used to get hot coffee and donuts," Alice read from her tourist booklet.

"Let me at them," said Fay.

"You're nearly a century late," laughed Alice.

Instead of coffee and donuts, the four women munched on peanuts and sipped ice water as they rested. Then May scrambled stiffly to her feet.

"Only three more miles," she said heartily. "Then we can have rice and tuna stew and bed."

"Saints preserve us, three more miles," Pat exclaimed.

"Not much bed on the ground," Fay complained. She was crouching by a tree stump on which her backpack was resting.

"En avant, mes amies," said Alice at last.

The four of them lined up and started off again along the track, walking more slowly than before. Alice began to count each step, shifting the pack after each fifty so that a new part of her body would begin hurting. What if I can't do it, after all, she thought. What'll I do? They'll all be mad at me and say I shouldn't have come. A feeling of panic swept over her. What if I fail?

"One foot and then the other," she heard her mother muttering to herself ahead of her. "God, if you'll pick them up, I'll put them down."

Alice began to concentrate on each foot. One forward, then the other. That wasn't too bad. She could keep that up for awhile. Her feeling of panic receded.

Alice was so numb that it took her a few seconds to look up and realize when they were finally at the end of the trail.

"Seven o'clock and we're here," May announced. "Canyon City. There used to be an aerial tramway which swung goods up the valley using steam boilers for power. We can visit the ruins after we've rested."

"Here at last," gasped Pat.

"Thank God," said Fay.

Gingerly Alice lowered her pack to the ground and looked about her. I don't think I can get through another day like this, she thought, before lowering herself to the ground like a rag doll.   What'll I do?

Chapter 4

Alice lay on the ground for half an hour, too exhausted to do more than wave a mosquito from her face now and then when its whining noise was louder than she could bear. She stirred only when May brought her a cup of what she called tea.

"There's no wood here so I had to heat the water on our cooking fuel. Heaven knows what it's made of, but it gives off almost no heat."

"It is rather pale," said Alice, looking at the tea. "I was going to say 'at least it's hot,' but the mug is barely warm." She cradled it in her hands, then took a sip. She made a face before she could stop herself. "Thanks very much."

"I don't know how we'll cook the rice when we can't get the water to boil," May said in a worried voice." Anyway, we're all right tonight, we have two cans of stew to open. It'll take awhile for them to warm up, so keep on resting. We can put up the tent after eating."

Alice felt stronger after drinking her tea-water, so she struggled to her feet and walked over to Pat and Fay, who had put up their tent and were now collapsed on the ground inside it.

"Pretty grim, eh?" said Alice.

"Worse than I thought," muttered Pat, opening one eye to look at her.

"I think your mum was a little optimistic about how easy the hike was," said Fay ruefully.

Alice left them to visit the small green outhouse. Then she poked about the log cooking cabin before touring the rest of the campsite. She visited first a high pole nailed to two trees. A rope swung from it which hikers could use to fasten their bags of food high above the reach of bears. Then suddenly she saw Mike struggling out of a tiny green tent set up on the far side of the opening.

"Hi," Alice called. "I wondered if we'd see you again."

"We didn't think we'd overdo the first day so we stopped about five," said Mike. "Beautiful country isn't it? How have you found the hike so far?"

"Not bad at all," Alice lied.

Mike smiled to himself. He had seen Alice arrive and collapse on the ground almost immediately. "I can feel it in my muscles, though," he said, stretching his arms out.

"Yes," Alice agreed heartily.

"If you have a minute, do you want to see something really amazing?"

Alice looked back at their campsite. Her mother was lying by the stew, and the others were still in their tent. "Sure," she said.

"It's this way." Mike lead Alice on the path they would take in the morning. About a quarter of a mile along, beside a high stump, he turned off the path to the left. Alice followed him.

"I heard a noise when I was strolling here a while ago and thought it was some sort of bird. I never did find out what it was, but when I got here I found this." He crouched down beside an enormous, moss-covered boulder and pulled out a rusty tin container from a natural hollow underneath it. Alice watched transfixed as he pried off the lid and pulled out two misshapen red objects. Alice took them and examined them closely. They had rotted to some extent, but they were obviously two red shoes, women's shoes. They had small buttons down the side, small trim heels, and jaunty leather bows.

"Wow," said Alice, turning them slowly in her hands. "Isn't that something! They must have been put here in 1898, the year of the Goldrush."

"I couldn't believe it. I would have thought they'd have rotted away, but I guess the tin kept them dry."

"Poor woman, having to leave behind her red shoes," said Alice thoughtfully.

"It would be a strange sort of woman who would bring red shoes on a Goldrush," Mike said, winking.

"I admire her spirit," said Alice, ignoring the wink.

They put the shoes back carefully where Mike had found them, because they both knew that by law nothing in the park could be removed or displaced. Then they pushed their way back to the trail.

"What was that $2,000 Fay mentioned on the ship? Tim and I couldn't figure out what she was talking about," Mike said as they sauntered toward the camp.

Alice glanced at Mike and was silent for a minute. "Nothing really," she laughed. "Just an in-joke among our group."

When they reached the campsite, Alice rejoined her friends who were sitting on the ground eating tepid stew from their mugs.

"Chow's on," said Pat heartily, handing Alice her portion.

"Looks good," said Alice, again noting that her mug was barely warm to the touch.

They munched away in silence until Alice remembered what Mike had found.

"I have something terrific to show you after dinner. Wait'll you see them. Mére, you 'll have to bring your camera."

"Animal, vegetable or mineral?" Pat asked, perking up.

"You'll see," Alice answered mysteriously.

After a dessert of instant pudding made with skim milk powder, served again in their mugs, they washed the few dishes in the fast-flowing Taiya river, put on new coats of insect repellent against the mosquitoes, and set out to follow Alice. There was no sign of Mike or Tim near their tents, so Alice did not have to worry that Mike would mind her showing off his find. They marched along the path to the stump, turned left, then gathered around the shoes which Alice produced with a triumphant gesture.

"Imagine, red shoes back then," Fay squealed. "They're gorgeous!"

"Not in bad condition, either, considering," said Pat. "It always annoys me that books about the Goldrush only talk about what the men did. There were lots of women here too. I've seen them in the photos that were taken. Imagine what guts they had to come here, in red shoes no less." She laughed, but she was serious.

May took the shoes to a clearing where the rich light of the evening sun fell on them. There she photographed them from many angles, lying first on the ground, and then on her blue neckerchief.

"Maybe nobody's seen these since their owner discarded them," she mused.

"I'll take a snap, too," said Fay.

May turned to her sharply. "You won 't get much detail with a Brownie," she said.

"You never know," Fay answered lightly.

When they had all admired and photographed the shoes to their hearts' content, Alice put them into the tin container and replaced it in the niche below the boulder.

"Good-bye, red shoes," she said.

Back at their campsite, they decided to turn in for the night, even though it was not yet dark. May and Alice wrestled to put up their two-person tent, Pat climbed into the other tent to arrange her gear, and Fay wandered about the campsite, waiting for Pat to settle down so she in turn could organize her possessions. When Fay neared Mike's and Tim's campsite, she found the two men there, happily eating rice and hash heated to boiling on their propane stove.

"Hi," she said. "Mind if I join you? I'm waiting for my tentmate to settle down."

"Please do," said Tim. "Nice evening."

"You're certainly going to eat better than we are," Fay said after a moment's silence. "We didn't want to have to carry a real stove like yours, so we're stuck with what amounts to fondue heaters. They don't give off any heat here, so heaven knows what they'll do when we get to the top of the Chilkoot Pass."

"As long as you don't have rice," Mike smiled.

"We do, though. We have lots of rice," said Fay. "At least we can use woodfires at Sheep Camp tomorrow."

"Say, Fay--hey that rhymes," began Mike. "On the ship you mentioned something about $2,000. What did you mean?"

"Oh, that," said Fay. She thought of May, and of May's insistence that somehow she must be the one to win the money. "It's a contest, put on by Alaska and the Yukon. They're offering $2,000 to the person who can produce the best 'Tourist Package' that can be used to promote tourism along the Goldrush Trail."

"Can anyone enter?" asked Tim.

"Sure," replied Fay. "You just have to produce your entry by Discovery Days in Dawson City."

"That's when we'll be there," said Tim.

"I know," said Fay. "May hopes to win the prize with her photographs. She's a professional. She teaches photography at the college in Edmonton where I work."

"Does the entry have to be photographs?" said Mike, who had no camera.

"No, anything will do, probably the more original the better."

Mike and Tim were finished eating, so Fay got up to go. "We'll see you later," she said.

"Good night," the men replied almost together.

Fay wandered back to her tent. "Good night," she called to May and Alice, who had finished erecting their tent and were now rolling out their sleeping bags inside it.

"I see Tim and Mike are here," May said coolly.

"Yes. Good night, sleep tight."

"Don't let the bugs bite," Alice retorted.

In ten minutes, Alice and the others were fast asleep, dreaming of red shoes, and physical torture, and finding gold. In a half an hour, the entire campsite was still.

In the morning, Alice and the others slept until seven, well past sun-up. Alice offered to make the porridge, an "instant" brand that cooked for almost an hour before it was edible, so the others wandered about amusing themselves. May spent the time photographing a disintegrating saddle and a broken frying pan she had found among the nearby ruins.

After eating, they dismantled their tents, packed up their gear, and headed on east.   There was no sign of where Mike and Tim had camped-- they must have packed up and left before Alice and the others were awake.

"Leave nothing but your footprints," Alice said to Fay, who was just ahead of her.

"I always liked that slogan," replied Fay.

After a few minutes Alice stopped to shift her backpack, which was slipping to the right. The others trudged forward out of sight. As she started on again, Alice saw the distinctive tree stump ahead of her that Mike had pointed out the evening before. One more look at the shoes, she said to herself. Just one more look.

She hurried into the bush, knelt down by the boulder and reached into the hollow where she had placed the tin the night before. When she pulled the tin out, it felt curiously light. When she had pried off the lid, she realized why. The container was empty.

Chapter 5

Alice was appalled. What should she do? Who could have taken them? It couldn't be a coincidence that they had lain undiscovered since the last century, only to be found by two sets of people on the same day. They must have been taken by someone in her group, or by one of the men.

Alice marched on determinedly, thinking so hard that she no longer noticed the weight on her back nor the stones or roots she had to negotiate. It wouldn't be her mother because her mother would never do such a thing. Could it be Pat? She was into things about women. Or Fay? But what would either do with the shoes? They could never let anyone see them as mementoes of the Gold Rush, because it was illegal to have such things. They all knew that.

She was quickly catching up to Fay, whose orange bubble mattress attached to the top of her pack she could see bobbing up and down among the trees ahead of her, so she began to walk more slowly. It was probably the men, who hadn't taken seriously the notice about leaving everything alone. But what would the men do with a pair of women's shoes? Unless, of course, they were planning somehow to use them for the contest.

They paused for lunch at Pleasant Camp, swatting away at mosquitoes that made the camp seem almost unpleasant. There was a German couple already there who had seen a bear across the tumbling Taiya River.

"Not big, ten years," the man told them unhelpfully.

"Was the bear black or brown?" Pat asked him slowly and loudly, as if he were deaf as well as unable to speak English.

"Grey," he replied. His wife smiled and nodded beside him.

"Grey," she echoed.

"Whatever it was, at least there's a river between us," said Pat.

"Thank heavens," May exclaimed.

Alice munched absent-mindedly on a cracker with cheese on it. Should she mention the shoes? If Fay or Pat had taken them, they would be aghast that she knew they were gone. It might ruin the friendly feelings that existed among them. And what good would it do? No one would want to go back now.

"Have some melted glacier," Fay said, handing Alice a bottle of water Fay had collected from the nearby river.

"Thanks," said Alice. She took a swig of the ice-cold water and continued thinking as she helped herself to the common supply of nuts and raisins set out on a rock.

If I mention the shoes, Mére will think the men took them, and she'll be even more against them than she already is, she said to herself. She decided to say nothing.

In the afternoon they continued their steady climb, usually upward through dark woods but often down again too along the winding path.

Alice's worry about the shoes was replaced by worry about her shoulders. They were incredibly sore. She tried walking with her hands supporting the backpack for fifty careful steps--they were now edging through a swamp where logs had been thrown down to give hikers a footing--then with her hands grasping the shoulder straps for fifty more. When she tried fifty steps with her arms dangling free, the pain in her shoulders was almost unbearable. How could thirty pounds seem so much like a ton?

All of them were glad to reach Sheep Camp in the middle of the afternoon. Before the Goldrush, this part of the valley had been used by hunters trying to kill mountain sheep on the snowy slopes above them. During the goldrush, sheep had wisely moved elsewhere, and never returned. Then the camp was composed of many houses and tents of people preparing the assault on the summit of the pass ahead of them. Since then, trees had grown up so that they couldn't see the pass. This was perhaps as well, a display told them, because in the Goldrush Days many people had turned back at this point, realizing the whole idea of a stampede up such a slope was foolish.

There were five parties planning to climb over the summit the next day, all apprehensive as they milled about the central log cabin preparing dinners. A woman and her young son and daughter, who had climbed over the pass and back that same day, increased their fears.

"Make sure you take small steps and don't become exhausted.   When you get hot, take off a layer or two of clothing, and when it starts to fog up, put on rain gear."

"But that means I'll be taking my pack on and off all the time," Alice protested. "I can't even get it up on my back without help."

"That means you have to stay together," the woman continued seriously. "If you pause to rest, make sure you put on another sweater. You mustn't get hypothermia."

"What's that?" said Alice.

"That's when your body temperature falls because you're too cold. You can become irrational and do silly things. It's very dangerous."

The women were quiet as they ate their dinner of rice and chicken bits, each wondering if she were up to the next day's demands.

"At least there won't be bears when we're so high," said Alice at last.

"Of course there are bears," said the woman. We saw a black one at the tree line three years ago."

"Thanks," said Alice, sighing.

They got up the next morning at six, so that the snow they would cross would not be as melted as it would be later on in the day. After a breakfast of porridge and granola bars, they set off on the upward path in single file. Alice's pack felt better than it had the day before, but the creeks they had to ford, the boulders they had to jump onto and off, and the roots they had to navigate made their work harder than ever. It wasn't hot, but soon Alice felt herself perspiring profusely in the still air of the forest. As she pushed forward behind Fay, her back bent double under the pack's weight, she noticed sweat dropping from her forehead to the path in front of her. Sometimes her nose dripped too--her handkerchief was lost somewhere in her pack--and once saliva drooled from her mouth.

"This is awful," she said to herself at this point, feeling like a pack animal rather than a human being.

Ahead of her, Fay was also having trouble. She had taken off her outer green sweater and was now stopping to take off her brown one too.

"I've never been so hot in my life," Fay gasped. "Why were we told to dress as if we were going to the north pole?"

"It gets cold at the summit," Alice said.

Fay ignored her. "I'm going to leave the green wool here by the path," she said, folding it neatly and placing it on a boulder. "It's too heavy to carry and I have enough other clothes."

"We're not supposed to leave anything behind," Alice protested. "We're even carrying our garbage with us."

"Someone will need this sweater eventually," Fay reasoned. "It's not new, but it's warm."

"But you can't just leave it here," Alice said again, horrified at what Fay was doing.

"Watch me," Fay replied. She slung her pack onto her back again and resumed her steady climb, leaving the green sweater where it was.

Alice looked at the sweater doubtfully. Perhaps she should take it, she thought, but she knew she couldn't manage to carry more weight. She grimaced, and plodded slowly forward without the sweater.

After an hour, they were above the tree line and could see what seemed to be the pass far above them, but which they had been assured by the woman the night before was really just a false summit. The real one lay beyond and far higher. The valley floor was strewn with boulders and patches of snow over and among which they slowly made their way forward, following from one stone cairn to the next. In the open here there was a cool wind, so they no longer felt hot, although the sun was brilliant above them. To the left was a high mountain from which an avalanche had killed scores of people at Sheep Camp in 1898, its summit now strewn with patches of snow. Nearby was a small hill topped by a tangle of old timbers, all that remained of an aerial system that had swung goods by wire from here to the summit.

After another hour of moving a short distance, resting to get their breath, then climbing on again, the four women crossed the false summit and reached Scales, at the foot of the Golden Stairs. It was here that men had lined up in the winter of '98 to climb the forty-five degree slope of snow into which the stairs had been cut, each carrying part of his ton of supplies which had to be piled at the summit before he would be allowed by the Royal Northwest Mounted Police into Canada.

"Why Scales?" Alice asked the others as they sat eating raisins for energy and contemplating what lay ahead.

"This was where they reweighed the goods of packers who were being paid to carry goods," Pat explained. "There was one rate for getting each pound this far, and then a higher rate for getting it from here to the summit."

"And we do it for nothing!" Alice laughed ruefully.

"Actually, we pay a good deal for doing it," said her mother. "Look at the train and boat fares and freeze-dried foods."

"How true," said Fay.

When they had sat down to rest, the sky had been a clear blue and they had been warm. Ten minutes later, the sky had clouded up and they were chilly. They all put on sweaters except Fay, who climbed off to the right to investigate the remains of a plane that had been wrecked several years ago.

"Come on, Fay. We're starting on," Pat called.

"I'll be right back," Fay answered.

A few minutes earlier the Golden Stairs had been clearly marked in its ascent toward the summit. Now they stood beside one orange marker peering ahead to see the next.

"You go first, you have sharp eyes," May said to Alice.

Alice inched her way upward, resting every twenty steps until she reached the next marker. Then she picked out the marker beyond and headed toward it. The others followed her, keeping within sight of each other except for Fay, who was slow returning from her attempt to reach the wreck of the airplane.

After twenty minutes they came to an even steeper patch of loose rocks and shale. Alice tried to climb carefully over this, but almost at once her foot broke loose a large rock that slid down toward May.

"For heaven's sake, watch what you're doing," shouted May, who fortunately had seen it coming and stopped it with her hand. "A rock like that could knock someone right off the hill."

"Sorry," said Alice. She resumed her climb even more slowly, using her feet and hands at each step. May, following her, dislodged another stone that slid narrowly past Pat's right hand.

"Sorry," said May. "It's easier to do than I thought."

Pat glared up at her, then looked around to see where Fay was. She was almost out of sight below her, with her brown sweater still wrapped around her waist.

"It's not too bad," she called down to her.

By the time Alice, May and Pat reached the top of the steepest section, it had begun to rain. They put on their rain suits quickly, for shelter against the wind as well as for keeping dry.

"You two go on," said Alice. "I'll wait for Fay." They could see her struggling upward below them.

Pat and May turned again to the slope, while Alice crouched beside a boulder trying to keep warm. She looked around her, in awe of what the

Stampeders must have encountered day after day. Sunny weather wasn't the norm on the summit; rain and fog were.

When Alice looked down again at Fay, she was horrified by what she saw. Fay had put on her brown sweater, but none of her rain gear. She had her backpack beside her on the ground and was rummaging through the contents, hunting for something. Rain was pouring down on her and on everything she had in her pack.

"What are you doing?" Alice called down urgently. "All your things are getting wet! You'll catch your death of cold!"

"I can't find my green sweater. It's made of wool," Fay called back. "I'm not going anywhere until I find it!"

Alice was aghast. Didn't Fay remember that she had left her green sweater far behind on the trail? In a panic Alice wondered what she should do. Fay seemed to have gone out of her mind. She could easily die right there on the hill with her clothes wet and in the cold wind.

Chapter 6

For a moment, Alice was too horrified to do anything as she watched rain pour down on Fay's clothing and sleeping bag. A wet sleeping bag, especially one made of down, was a major catastrophe in the northland. A moment before she had been almost afraid to look back, the ground was so steep below her where Fay still searched hopelessly for her green wool sweater. Now she realized that she was the one who would have to go down and help Fay, since Pat and May were already out of sight above her.

Alice took off her own backpack and wedged it against a boulder. Then, pressing her stomach against the ground, she began slowly to descend toward Fay. She moved one foot at a time, carefully feeling out a toe grip that would hold her weight before moving her other foot or hands. She was terrified that she might dislodge a rock that would tumble down and hit Fay, who was paying no attention to her would-be rescuer. Inch by inch she crept downward until she was beside Fay, who now looked at her in surprise.

"What are you doing down here?" she said. "I thought you'd be at the summit by now. I'll be right along, as soon as I find my sweater. I'm frozen." Fay's teeth chattered as she spoke.

"We have to get going before you get any colder," Alice said encouragingly. "Come on, we'll put on your rain gear and finish the climb. It's not much farther."

"I'm cold," wailed Fay. "Where is my sweater!"

"You left your sweater behind. Remember how hot you were before?"

Fay looked at Alice without understanding what she was saying.

"I'm cold," she repeated.

"Your rain gear will keep out the cold," said Alice. "Here, let me help you."

Alice took Fay's rubber poncho out of her pack and drew it over Fay's head. Then she stuffed Fay's belongings back into the backpack. She swung it over her own back and began the careful climb upward again, this time stopping with each step to make sure that Fay was following her. If she wasn't, she reached out and took Fay's hand and partly pulled her upward. The strain on Alice was immense. She began to sweat under her heavy clothing, even though Fay continued to shiver.

When the two reached Alice's backpack, Alice decided they should rest.

"We're nearly there," she told Fay.

"I'm still cold," Fay shivered, her words slurring together.

Alice changed her mind. No matter how exhausted they were they had better continue while Fay was capable of it. Her movements were already becoming clumsy. Alice detoured around her backpack, soaking wet in the rain, and continued to guide Fay slowly upward. At last, after what seemed like hours, she spotted her mother crouching beside a boulder trying to keep out of the rain. "Give us a hand," she shouted. "Fay's pretty cold and wet."

May looked over in amazement to see Alice leading Fay toward the summit with Fay's backpack on. She realized at once that this was an emergency.

"Hold on," she called through the rain. "I'm coming." She put down her own pack and ran over to join them.

"Here, let me help," she gasped, putting her arm around Fay. Together, Alice and her mother urged Fay forward, almost encircling her with their arms.

When they reached the summit of the Chilkoot Pass, the rain was so heavy they didn't see Pat come up until she was almost on them. Like May, she had been resting at the summit.

"What's wrong?" she asked.

"Fay's cold and wet. We've got to get her to Stone Crib as fast as possible." Stone Crib had two A-shaped windowless huts about half a mile from the summit, each so small that it held six people at most, none of them standing.

"You lead the way," Pat said to Alice whom she could see was exhausted. "May and I will bring Fay." Fay was barely' conscious by this time, her legs and arms moving erratically as the other two half dragged her along.

"I'm cold," she said in a slurred voice.

"We'll be in a hut in a few minutes," May told her. "Try and walk properly so we can get there sooner."

The small brigade moved slowly down the valley to Stone Crib, their way indicated by a succession of orange flags. When they were nearly there they were met by an American Ranger just emerging from one of the small huts. He stared at the women in surprise.

"What's up?" he asked.

"I think Fay here has hypothermia," Pat answered. "We've got to get her warm."

"This is serious," said the Ranger, noting Fay's almost unconscious form. "Bring her into this hut. I'll bring over my Coleman Lamp so we can see what we're doing and have some warmth."

They heaved Fay into the first hut, then crawled in after her. There was scarcely room for them all.

"Take off her wet clothes and put on dry ones," the Ranger ordered. "And get her into a sleeping bag."

"All her clothes are wet," Alice groaned, struggling out of Fay's backpack which she had carried so far.

"Oh, no," said Pat. "In the excitement we left our packs at the summit. There are dry clothes in them, and dry sleeping bags."

"Well, get her clothes off and wrap her in this old blanket. I'm going to radio to the Canadian Warden for help. I have to go back to Sheep Camp where there's a broken leg."

"Are we in Canada now?" asked Alice.

"The border's at the summit."

"What else shall we do?" asked Pat.

"Rub her hands and feet and give her hot drinks every half hour or so. We've got to get her warm again. Get your stove out and start heating water for tea."

"The stove's in my pack," said Pat in a small voice.

"Get with it," said the Ranger. "This is an emergency!"

"You," he said to Alice, "you come with me to the summit and bring back dry clothes. You two get her wet things off and start rubbing her hands and feet. I'll go and radio the Canadian Warden."

He stamped out of the hut, banging the door after him. Pat and May began working on Fay, who seemed now to be asleep, while Alice put on her dripping rain gear again. The lamp cast eerie shadows on the ceiling while the rain poured down and the wind whistled outside. None of them spoke for awhile. Then Alice said, "I'll be off then."

"Hurry back, love," said May. "Don't get lost."

The march back to the summit was nearly as slow as the march from it. Now there was no ailing person to lead, but the path was uphill and the wind strong against Alice and the Ranger. They pressed through the rain in single file, both trying to keep their footing on the slippery ground. At the summit, the Ranger held Pat's backpack while Alice slid her arms through the straps. Then he said, "Follow the flags carefully, but hurry. Her life could be in danger. The Canadian Warden was at Deep Lake Campsite so she should be here before too long."

He turned on his heel and strode on toward Sheep Camp.

"Good luck," he called over his shoulder, as if as an afterthought.

Alice retraced the path carefully toward Stone Crib. Before Fay had come down with hypothermia, she had felt exhausted, hardly able to put one foot above the other. Now she felt exhilarated, on an important mission, eager to save lives. She felt entirely confident that she could walk as quickly as anyone, and find the way as surely. Within twenty minutes she was back at the hut.

"Here's dry clothing," she said as she entered. In the flickering light Pat and May were sitting ·on the floor beside Fay, who was still unconscious.

"Good. Give me the stove while May gets out my sleeping bag," said Pat.

"I'll go back for another pack," said Alice.

"No, it's too dangerous," objected her mother.

"We could use the other sleeping bag," said Pat.

"Will you be careful, then?" asked May.

"Of course," said Alice, "I'll be back before you know it."

By now the rain was slacking off, so this trip of Alice's was easier than the one before. She picked up her mother's pack this time and was back at the hut within forty minutes.

Fay was still lying helpless between Pat and May, but it seemed hopeful to have her snugly arranged in a sleeping bag. The uncontrollable shivering which had overtaken her at intervals had stopped. Alice left her dripping rain gear outside as she entered the hut.

"I could make another trip to get my bag," she said doubtfully. The warmth of the room suddenly reminded her that she was exhausted.

"We'll go later," said her mother. "You lie down for awhile now. You've done enough."

Alice lay down for a minute, but was asleep almost instantly. She was only awakened several hours later by the arrival of the Warden, and behind her Tim and Mike.

"Sorry to hear about Fay," Mike whispered to Alice, who had sat up and was rubbing her eyes. "Will she be all right?"

"I think so," replied Alice softly. "She was pretty bad."

The Warden had taken in at a glance what was happening. "That stove is ridiculous," she said loudly. "You have to keep giving someone with hypothermia hot fluids. Those fondue heaters are no good at all. What have you given her?"

"Some tea. And some hot chocolate," said May.

"Made with boiling water?" demanded the Ranger.

"I guess not," replied May.

"I'm glad Mike brought theirs then," said the Ranger.

As if on cue, Mike unearthed his propane stove from his pack, lit it and placed the pan of water on it.

"We'll have boiling water in no time," he said.

"Hypothermia is a dangerous condition," the Ranger lectured the women, as if they didn't already know that. "The patient must be kept warm and must be given hot drinks as often as possible."

The night passed in a daze for Alice. She slept most of the time, rousing herself occasionally to watch May or Pat holding Fay's head so that she could drink tea or soup. When May was on duty, Pat slept beside Alice on the floor. When Pat was making tea, it was May who napped beside her. The Ranger and the men had gone.

By the next morning, Fay was out of danger. She was alert and warm, apologizing for all the trouble she had caused them. The four of them were still tired, so they dozed all morning. Outside the sun was shining again, so that soon they were able to turn off the lamp and open the door to let in natural light. Fay had felt well enough to lay out her wet clothes and sleeping bag on the porch to dry. Was her refusal to allow the others into her bag connected with the red shoes, Alice wondered? It seemed a mean thought, when Fay had been so ill.

When they finally roused themselves to make lunch, Alice was astonished to see her backpack in the corner by the door.

"Who brought it here?" she asked. She had been afraid she would have to go back over the summit and part way down the Golden Stairs to get it. The thought had depressed her when she remembered the steepness of the slope and the unstableness of the rocks.

"Mike and Tim, I think," said Pat.

"That was really good of them," replied Alice.

"They left to go back to Deep Lake as soon as they saw Fay was going to be all right."

After lunch, Fay said that she felt well enough to begin hiking again. It was warm outside, so there was no danger of her becoming chilled. They divided Fay's clothing among them so that Fay's load was much lighter than usual, and set out about two o'clock.

The first part of the afternoon's hike was along a line of lakes which formed the headwaters of the Yukon River. The water in them was a clear emerald blue. After Happy Camp, the trail began winding over a high hill, through and around immense boulders. They were still above the tree line, so they continued to have a fine view over the lakes to their left and beyond to snow-spotted mountains. When Deep Lake was just visible in the distance, they had an accident that must be one in a lifetime. As they progressed single-file toward the north, Alice, who was leading, came around a bend to find herself face to face with a bull moose. The sound of rushing water in a nearby fast-flowing stream had masked the noise made by both parties. The moose without hesitation swung to the right and plunged down the hill. Alice, with a gasp, took a step back, tripped over a rock, and fell to the ground in a heap.

Chapter 7

The others stopped in their tracks when they saw the moose suddenly appear before them. No one said anything as Alice tripped and fell, or as the moose trotted with long strides down the hill. Then they reacted with a buzz of comments.

"Oh Alice, are you all right," May exclaimed bounding forward as well as she could with her heavy pack on to give Alice a hand up.

"A moose! Right above the tree line!" said Pat.

"I've never seen a moose before," Fay squealed.

"I'll be all right," Alice answered May, struggling to her feet and bending her ankle back and forth. "He just startled me really. A moose was the last thing I expected to meet."

They all gathered around Alice, looking at her extended foot.

"Will it hold your weight?" asked Pat.

"Yes. I'll just have to take extra care where I put my feet," said Alice. She started off along the path again, going steadily as before but more slowly.

The foursome followed the trail past Deep Lake, above the canyon joining Deep Lake and Lake Lindeman, and finally reached the latter in the early evening. They were all exhausted, Alice especially so because of her injured foot. They decided to sleep in the cookhouse rather than put up their tents, so they spread out their bubble mattresses and sleeping bags and carried cooking and wash water up from the lake while Pat heated up two cans of pork and beans. It was after nine, so they were the only hikers still using the log hut. They sat on benches around the wall to eat.

"I've never been more tired in my life," Fay said as she slowly spooned beans from her cup to her mouth. "I'm almost too tired to eat."

"Me too," said Alice.

"Tomorrow will be an easy day," May soothed them. "We won't have to leave here for Bare Loon Lake until about three. You'll have all morning and early afternoon to do what you want."

Right after dinner, without washing the dishes, they wriggled into their sleeping bags on the floor and were asleep before the fire in the stove had begun to die down.

After breakfast the next day, the four of them walked over to a tent displaying old pictures of Lindeman City, as their campsite was known in the spring of 1898. At that time 10,000 people camped in tents, building boats and waiting for the ice to go out so they could follow it to the goldfields of the Klondike. The pictures of the city and of other parts of the Chilkoot trail thrilled them.

"Here's an Indigenous woman carrying a sheet iron stove over the trail!" said Pat.

"And here's where we climbed the Golden Stairs," said Alice.

"Look, they had a chute the men slid on down to the bottom of the hill again, after they lugged each load to the summit."

May poked Alice and motioned toward Fay. She didn't want Alice to remind Fay of how she had broken down there. Alice winced and turned quickly to the next picture.

"Here are some goats pulling a sleigh," she said.

They spent half an hour reliving history, then spread out over the campsite to look at the old things left by the Stampeders. Everywhere they went were long rusted nails, bits of tins, broken glass, parts of shoes, and occasionally a broken sledge.

Alice wandered among some permanent tents used by the Warden and by young people working in the area, then crossed over to the second cook-house at the far side of the campsite. There, to her pleasure, she found Mike sunbathing in shorts by the lake and Tim photographing an assortment of old tins. He was rearranging them carefully in a haphazard way, then taking their pictures at three different exposures.

"Don't you get bored doing that?" Alice asked.

Tim laughed. "You can get surprising effects," he said, squinting at his most recent design.

"Thanks so much for bringing my backpack to Stone Crib," Alice said to Mike.

"No problem," Mike replied, stretching his arms.

"I'm just wandering about," Alice said, hoping Mike might join her, but he had already closed his eyes.

"Have fun," he said.

Alice walked along a wooded path that used to be the main street of Lindeman City. Only blue-marked stakes showed where the various streets had been. At Sourdough marker she found Pat sitting on a log, apparently thinking.

"There were a few log cabins here," Pat said. "I guess a few of the women must have slept there, as well as in the tents."

"Hmm," said Alice, not wanting to be drawn into a conversation on women.

"Some were laundresses, I think, and some ran restaurants," Pat continued. She made a notation in her notebook.

"Lunch is at one," Alice said as she sauntered on.

Alice met her mother beside the signpost pointing the way from where they had come. Like Tim, she too was absorbed in taking a number of shots at various times and exposures.

"The professional at work," Alice commented.

"I hope so," May laughed. The light was perfect so she felt happy.

The signpost pointed also to the cemetery, so Alice strolled there next. It was on a hill above the campsite, with a lovely view over the lake to the mountains beyond. Here she came upon Fay, sitting on a boulder sketching the scene below her. Alice glanced at her work.

"I didn't know you were such a good artist," she said.

"Thanks," Fay replied. "I've always loved to draw. I took lessons in high school."

"Lunch at one," Alice called back after she had looked at some of the graves, each surrounded by a high fence and with a wooden marker so weathered that no name was still visible. On a central monument she had read part of a poem by Robert Service, his tribute to the Yukon, the land he had loved.

As Alice returned to the cookhouse to make lunch, she thought about the men who had died here in the search for gold. No one even knew their names anymore. No one knew where they had come from, nor how they died. Yet Robert Service's poetry lived on.

After eating lunch and packing up their belongings, the four women set off on the three-mile hike to Bare Loon Lake. The trail was beautiful, high on the right shore of Lake Lindeman at first, then across rock outcropping and through woods to their new campsite. Alice half expected to see Mike and Tim camped there, but they had apparently not stopped on their way out to the railroad. The women pitched their tents on sandy soil above the mountain lake while Fay made macaroni and cheese on their small stove.

"It may seem unhiker-like to use a stove," she apologized, "but a sign over there says "No Wood Fires." I guess they're afraid of forest fires, it's been so dry this summer."

After they had eaten sitting on rocks admiring a not-bare loon floating on the water, Pat washed the dishes. As she scrambled down to the lake to throw out the dirty wash water, replete with bits of macaroni, May called out "Don't throw it in the lake. That pollutes it."

"But fish love macaroni," Pat said. "I always give them leftovers for dinner."

"You shouldn't," May countered. "Conservationists are very careful not to pollute lakes nowadays. You can't have camped for awhile."

"No," Pat agreed, feeling annoyed.

She scrambled up toward the tents again and was about to fling the water onto the ground when Fay yelled out "Not on the ground! You'll attract bears!"

"What shall I do with the stupid water," Pat said angrily. "It has to go somewhere."

"You can put it down the latrine pit," Alice said. "That's what I had to do at Lindeman's."

Pat marched off with the water muttering "Conservationists! Bears!" until she was out of hearing. Alice was reminded of the joke about why guns were not allowed on the Canadian section of the Chilkoot Trail--so that hikers wouldn't shoot each other when they drove each other mad.

Their final day on the trail was a short one. The winding nature of the forest path was familiar to them, but now frequent boggy patches soon soaked their shoes through. After a mile, they reached the railroad line which runs between Skagway and Whitehorse, crossing the coastal mountain range by the White Pass. Years before, when the railroad was running, Chilkoot hikers could be picked up at the Bennett Station. Now they had to walk five miles down the railroad line to the highway where they could catch a bus to Whitehorse.

The women's march down the railroad was uneventful until mile 36 noted by the numbers in orange on a telegraph post. Their food was nearly gone so their packs were less heavy, though in any case their muscles were more used to the weights they carried. Suddenly Pat stumbled over a railway tie and stopped dead, staring ahead.

"Look," she hissed, "a grizzly! There, in the bushes to the left!"

They all came abreast of her and stared where she was pointing. Sure enough, there was a large grizzly sniffing about near the track they were following. On the right side of the track, the ground fell steeply to a marshy area far below them. There was no way to go on except near the grizzly.

"What'll we do," whispered Alice. "I'm not going anywhere near that bear!"

"Come on back a way," said May. "We'll wait until it goes away."

They backed up slowly, all eyes glued to the bear, which seemed not to have seen them. When they were well around the first corner, they took off their packs and sat down on the rails to wait.

"We'll give him fifteen minutes," said May.

"Or maybe it's a female with cubs?" suggested Pat.

"Not that, please," sighed Alice. She knew how dangerous mother bears could be.

They decided to wait half an hour, passing the time by peeling and slowly eating their two last oranges. When they ventured forward again, there was no sign of the bear. They walked stiffly by the place where the bear had been, Alice and May together, then Pat and Fay, none daring to look to the left. When they were well past, Alice laughed in relief, but when she glanced back there was the grizzly again, sniffing about the tracks.

"Don't look now, but she's still there," she exclaimed in a low voice.

"We mustn't panic," gasped Fay.

"We'll all walk on normally," ordered May.

They moved on quietly, staring ahead, listening hard. Five minutes later, when they looked back again and saw no sign of the animal, they finally relaxed.

"Bears are no match for us women," Pat said proudly.

"We were just lucky," Alice replied.

They walked on to the highway and from there took the bus to Whitehorse, past emerald green and long narrow lakes bordered by lovely rounded mountains. Outside the city the bus let them off at the Robert Service Campground, where they would stay the night. It had been a long day, so they were content with a dinner of bread and cheese. Before long they had pitched their tents, rolled out their sleeping bags, and were fast asleep.

For some reason, Alice didn't know why, she awoke about two o'clock and decided to sit up and put on her wool socks. She had just laid down again when she heard the sound of someone running toward their tents. She listened with interest as the sounds grew nearer. Suddenly the steps were almost at their tent. They stopped. There was an instant's silence and Alice felt a heavy weight fall on her, crushing the breath out of her lungs. Just as suddenly, she felt the weight removed and heard a Tarzan-like yell, the like of which she had never heard before.

"Aaaeeee!"

Chapter 8

Dead silence followed the wild scream. Then the man pounded away toward the highway, leapt into a car and slammed the door. The car, which must have been waiting for him there at the road, took off at high speed toward Whitehorse.

"What was that?!" gasped Pat, waking from a sound sleep and sitting up in her sleeping bag.

"Just some idiot fooling around," mumbled Fay turning over. "Go back to sleep."

"What was it," Pat persisted, wiggling out of her bag and pulling on her jeans.

When she unzipped the door of the tent and looked out, she gasped with horror. The other tent was completely flattened, except for two bumps which must be May and Alice.

"I'll look after it in the morning," Fay muttered, sinking back into sleep.

Pat rushed to her friends and lifted up what had been the door. "May, Alice, are you all right? What happened?"

Slowly the two bodies began to move, breaking out of their shock.

"That man must have jumped on us on purpose! Alice, are you okay?" May asked.

Alice stretched herself gingerly. "My side hurts where he landed, and my arm, but the rest of me feels fine."

"What a yahoo," May exclaimed angrily. "Imagine hurting someone you don't even know!"

"Are you all right?" Pat asked May, who by now had managed to unzip the door and struggle out of the debris.

"I'm fine. I just felt a heavy weight suddenly, and then the scream. What shall we do now?" May was beginning to shiver, Pat did not know from cold or from shock. Mosquitoes were buzzing all around her bare arms and legs.

"The first thing is to get you warm again," Pat said. "You get back into your sleeping bag and I'll rig up the tent so it will do for the night. Should we go to the hospital about your arm and side?" she asked Alice.

Alice looked out bleakly at the mosquitoes and at her mother' s shivering form.

"I'll stay here 'til morning," she decided. "I'd rather just lie here." She felt completely drained of energy.

May clambered back into the morass of blue nylon, found her sleeping bag and slid into it.

"I'm frozen," she said, her teeth clenched.

Pat decided not to worry about the end of the tent. which was lying on Alice's and May's legs. Instead, she made a small tripod from unbroken pieces of the ridgepole, tied them together with the cord from the tent case, and draped the front of the tent over it so that May and Alice would have some room for their heads. Then she spread out the sides of the tent and anchored them with stones.

"At least the netting isn't touching you so you'll be free of mosquitoes, if you don't thrash about too much," Pat said. She looked at the moon above, sending pale light through the trees. "It probably won't rain anyway."

When she was sure that May and Alice were as comfortable as she could make them, Pat returned to her tent where Fay lay sleeping soundly.

Neither Alice nor May slept for the rest of the night, but they didn't speak either. What could they say? Each lay wrapped in thoughts of what had happened. When they heard Pat and Fay getting up about seven o'clock, Alice spoke for the first time.

"I was lying on my side. He must have pushed my arm into my ribs when he landed."

"I was on my stomach, lower down I guess."

"I heard him running toward the tent, I must have been half asleep, so at least I realized what was happening," said Alice.

"His body was what woke me," said May. "We'll have to see about your arm and side this morning. We'll go to the hospital."

"What if we'd been sitting up in the tent?" Alice asked. "I'd sat up about five minutes before he came, to put socks on, 'cause my feet were cold. He could have broken my back." She felt sick at the thought.

"He could have killed us," May said. "We'll go to the police first, but how could they ever find out who did it?"

Fay made breakfast while Pat and May studied the blue tent to see what was broken. Alice watched them. All of the white tent struts were bent out of shape, and one of the segments of the ridgepole was snapped through.

"We'll buy a new segment today," said Pat. "It could be worse. We can still use the struts."

When Pat went for water at the communal tap some distance away, May followed her.

"I'm worried," May said. "What if Alice can't paddle? What'll we do?"

"She isn't in much pain, she says," replied Pat, "so I doubt if anything's broken. Her ribs are probably bruised."

"But can she paddle?"

"It won't matter the first thirty miles, the current will take us along. Lake Laberge is something else, though." They watched the water pour into the pot Pat held in silence. Would they be able to finish the trip?

"Well, let's not worry until we see what the doctor says," Pat said as they returned to their tents.

When they had cleaned up the campsite, the four of them took a taxi into town. Pat and Fay got off at Main Street to go shopping, while May and Alice continued on to the hospital.

The woman at the hospital who took information about patients could scarcely believe what May told her.

"You mean a man belly-dived right onto your tent in the middle of the campsite in the middle of the night?"

"Exactly," said May.

"But that's awful! You could have been killed."

"We know," said Alice.

"Some people in Whitehorse are pretty dumb," the woman continued, "but this is ridiculous." She shook her head in wonder from side to side as she wrote down the details.

The doctor who examined Alice was equally bemused.

"What are we coming to when something like this happens," she said as she pressed down against each of Alice's ribs and examined her arm.

"The arm's okay, just bruised, but I'd like to have an X-ray of those ribs. There's no serious damage, your heart and lungs are all right. You're lucky he wasn't heavier."

After the X-ray, the technician told May and Alice to come back after lunch for the result, since the doctor had a call to make at the hot springs during the morning. They took a taxi back to the police station to report the attack. The police officer they talked to was as astonished as the woman at the hospital had been.

"You mean he just leapt on your tent? For no reason? Did he know who you were?"

"I don't think so," said May. "How could he? He had a car, and campers usually don't."

"It was unprovoked," the officer muttered as he wrote down the details May gave him.

Alice began to feel pleased with herself, the center of so much attention.

"If we'd been sitting up, he could have killed us," she said.

"You're not kidding," replied the officer. "I'm afraid we won't catch the man, though, with no other evidence. Odd things often happen in the Yukon, as you'll find on your canoe trip."

"If we take the trip," said May grimly. "We have to see what the doctor says about Alice's ribs. We'll be back anyway before we leave town."

Alice felt deflated again. What if this meant she couldn't paddle? What if the trip was ruined for everyone? She couldn't bear to think of it.

"Let's go and have a soft drink at that restaurant," she said.

"Yes, let's. Now don't worry. Everything will turn out for the best."

While May and Alice were at the hospital and the police station, Fay and Pat wandered along the main streets. When they came to the magnificent new Yukon administration building, they decided to go in. Once inside, they were overwhelmed by the modern design and the pictures lining the walls.

"These paintings are almost all by women," Pat said when she had scrutinized each in turn. "That's amazing. In the rest of the country they mostly hang paintings by men." In the art gallery, too, which formed one room of the building, almost all of the art was by women.

"Women are very creative in the Yukon," the attendant told them, delighted at their enthusiasm. "You must see the tapestries which hang next door." She directed the women to the legislative room where five huge hangings extending two stories lined one wall. Four of them represented the seasons, and the fifth "Survival". Each featured women doing various everyday Yukon activities, their faces left blank so that they represented all women.

Back outside, Pat directed their route to the nearest book and stationary store, which they both entered eagerly.

"I'm going to buy any books they have about Yukon women," Pat announced. "They're creative and strong. The world needs to know more about them--we could learn a thing or two."

"I'm going to buy some pencil crayons," said Fay. "I want to draw some of the things we're seeing. They're unique."

Ten minutes later, the two women met at the cash register. Fay had a set of pencil crayons and another of charcoal sticks to buy. Pat had six books by or about Yukon women.

"We'll spread the gospel about the Yukon," Fay laughed.

"No ulterior motive?" teased Pat. "Like $2,000?" Fay looked at her, startled. "Of course not."

They both burst out laughing as they paid the cashier, each looking about casually to see if May was anywhere near.

Chapter 9

Alice and the others met for lunch at the No Pop shop.

"We've been to the new Government Building," Fay said as they munched on their sesame seed bun sandwiches. "And we've bought some books about the Yukon and some postcards."

"We weren't sure what maps to buy to take on the river," Pat added. "We should all go and decide which are best this afternoon."

"If we go on the trip," said May glumly.

"What do you mean?" asked Fay. "You said Alice's side wasn't serious. Why wouldn't we go?"

They all looked at May with worried eyes. "The doctor said it wasn't serious, but that was because the ribs weren't forced into the lungs or heart. There's a difference between serious and being able to paddle for two weeks, especially across Lake Laberge."

"My ribs don't feel too bad now, mére," Alice said. "I'm sure I'll be fine."

"We'll see what the doctor says this afternoon. If the worst comes to the worst, Alice can sit in my canoe and rest and I can paddle alone. I've often done that."

"What about Lake Laberge?"

There was silence at the table. They all knew that with the current running at four knots or more along most of the Yukon River they would reach Dawson City some time, even if they didn't paddle at all. Lake Laberge was different, though. It was only thirty miles below Whitehorse, and was itself thirty miles long. There was no current there to speed them on their way. They would have to paddle the entire distance. What was worse, it was such a shallow lake that sudden winds could whip up high waves in a matter of minutes.

Unless their canoes stayed close to shore, they could capsize and die of cold before they reached shore.

"Well, we'll see what the doctor says," replied Pat eventually.

They planned to meet at the Tourist Center at three o'clock. Fay and Pat went off to buy stamps at the Post Office, while Alice and May returned by taxi to the hospital.

The doctor had already examined the X-rays and was waiting for them. "As I suspected, the one rib is cracked, which isn't serious. I'll tape up your chest, and you can take it easy for a couple of days. It will heal by itself in no time."

"What about paddling?" asked Alice nervously.

"I'd give it a miss for two or three days, but after that it should be no problem. I treated a fisherman last year who could paddle fine even with three cracked ribs. It didn't hurt at all, he said. What did hurt was lifting heavy things. So go easy on that."

"You heard her," Alice grinned at her mother, relieved that she would be able to paddle and amused that she wouldn't be able to shift gear in and out of the canoes at each campsite.

"We can't afford to wait too long, though," said May in a worried voice. "We have to be in Dawson City for Discovery Days, which is only sixteen days away. We should start the day after tomorrow if we hope to get there for sure."

"Do you have two to a canoe?" asked the doctor.

"Yes, Alice will bow and I'll stern," answered May.

"My daughter is home from university on holiday," the doctor said suddenly. "Would you like her to paddle in your canoe the first day? She's a whiz. She could paddle down to Lake Laberge instead of Alice. There's a cabin there, and a trail she can hike out on back to the highway. That will give Alice another day of rest."

May and Alice were delighted with this plan.

Without wasting a minute, the doctor phoned her daughter, Helen, and made the arrangements.

"Helen thinks that's a great idea. It'll give her a day on the river and help you out at the same time. She says she'll meet you at the canoe rental office at ten o'clock, the day after tomorrow. She knows the man who runs it and she can help get your gear and the canoes over to the place where you'll leave from, beside the old railway station."

The doctor taped Alice up, and then they returned to the Tourist Center. Fay was already there, writing post cards to her friends back in Edmonton, and Pat came up several minutes later. She had found the Women's Center and had been talking to two old-time Yukoners.

May explained the new plan to the others, who were quite willing to postpone their start for a day and to have Helen join them.

"That was one terrific doctor," Pat exclaimed.

"An extra day will work out well," Fay commented. "We can buy our food supplies tomorrow, and visit the Museum too."

The next day was such a full one that they began to feel they could not have done without it. They slept again in the Robert Service Campground but spent the entire day in town. The canoe rental company agreed to the day's postponement; then they called the Mounted Police headquarters to leave the names and addresses of their next-of-kin in case they never reached Dawson City.

"It makes you think," said Pat as she filled out her page.

"Better safe than sorry," said the police officer. "It's important that you check in at Carmacks as you go through, that's two hundred miles downstream, and again at Dawson City when you get there. If you don't, we'll think you're in trouble and send out help. And that's expensive."

"My next of kin is you, mére," laughed Alice. "That won't help much if we're both eaten by bears."

"Put down your father," May said. "I'll put him down, too. Surely he'll be some use in an emergency."

"I'll make out a fire permit for your party, too," said the officer. "You can camp anywhere along the river, but always make sure your fire is out when you leave. We've had a dry summer so far, and we don't want any forest fires."

"Can we cut wood for fires?" asked Pat.

The officer laughed. "One thing there's no shortage of in the Yukon is firewood. There's dry drift wood everywhere along the river. I wouldn't bother even taking an axe."

After leaving the police station, they spent the rest of the morning at the Museum, studying their route on a large map and admiring old photographs taken during the Goldrush. Outside the Museum, they saw the cabin that a Sam McGee lived in, made famous because of Robert Service's poetry, and various vehicles that had been in use so many years ago. May spent a long time photographing the various exhibits, and Fay snapped several too. Pat browsed among the displays that dealt with women--their clothing, the stoves they cooked on, the old-fashioned piano they played.

Before lunch, May left the others to buy film at a camera store. As she was browsing among the camera supplies at the back of the store, something she loved to do, she saw Tim and Mike enter the store and go up to the service desk. They did not notice her.

"What are the chances of getting slides developed in a hurry in Dawson City," Tim asked the woman at the counter.

"Slight," she answered. "You can get prints done in a day or so, but not slides. They have to be sent to the lab."

"I'll have five rolls of colour prints then," said Tim.

"Why don't you get more than that?" Mike suggested. "There's no point possibly running out. Too much is at stake."

"Okay, make that eight," agreed Tim.

May watched the transaction from behind a stand of flash bulbs, appalled. "They must know about the contest. Damn!"

"Will that be all then?" the saleswoman asked the men, handing Tim his change.

"Yes, thanks. But wish us luck."

"Good luck," she replied, smiling.

After they had gone, May tried to buy ten rolls of colour prints for herself, but there were only four left.

"Everyone seems to be into prints, today," the woman laughed. "You can buy more rolls just down the street."

May was able to buy six more rolls at a second shop, but she did so with misgiving. Tim had an expensive camera she had seen, and he might know how to use it properly. How annoying it all was. How did they find out about the contest? She went to lunch feeling and looking grim.

In the afternoon, before shopping, Pat paid five dollars so she could pan for gold at a booth set up near the old station. She was given a large flat pan loaded with at least ten pounds of dirt and seeded with gold.

"You pay less if the dirt isn't seeded," the man who ran the booth explained to Pat. "That just means we put gold into the dirt so you're bound to strike it rich."

They all watched while Pat immersed the pan into a large tank of water. Slowly she shook the pan about so that bits of dirt fell into the water. When she was tired, she let May and Fay help, too. The pan was too heavy for Alice, with her cracked rib, to hold.

After ten minutes of timid splashing about and laughing by the three women, the owner came over to them laughing too.

"You'll never get to the gold at that rate," he chuckled. He took the pan from Fay and gave it a few mighty shakes. Dirt flew into the water on all sides.

"Like this," he said. "Gold is heavy. It'll stay at the bottom." Pat tried again, more boldly this time, followed by May and Fay.

After half an hour, only a small layer of dirt remained in the pan. The owner came over again and gave the pan to Alice.

"You try now," he said. "See those bright specks there? That's gold!"

Alice slopped out a little more of the dirt, and then Pat took the last turn. Then the owner removed the specks with tweezers and put them in a tiny vial for Pat.

"See? I told you you'd be lucky," he said.

"All that work for this!" said Alice, staring at the tiny bits of gold. Indeed the vial magnified their size and made them look bigger than they really were.

Pat put the vial in her pocket. "You're just envious of my riches," she smiled.

Before they crossed the street to begin buying their groceries, the four of them paused to look out over the huge Yukon River rushing past them through the middle of the city. It was a lovely sunny day, and the sparkling water seemed to beckon to them.

Suddenly Alice pointed. "Look, there's Mike and Tim. They must be just leaving."

"Mike!" she yelled, waving her hands. "Bon voyage!"

Mike and Tim turned to look toward her.

"Bye for now," they called. "Take care!"

Soon the current had rushed them out of sight. "I guess we won't see them again," Alice said.

"Maybe in Dawson City," Fay replied.

Alice thoughtfully watched them go. Did the red shoes go with them in their packs? Or were they in their own party? She wished she knew.

The women themselves set out the following day at noon. Helen had been optimistic about an earlier start. It had taken them hours to pay for the canoes, arrange where to leave them in Dawson City, cart their gear by taxi from the campsite to the tour office, and truck it again from there to the launching site. While they loaded the canoes, Pat bought some fried chicken from a store across the street so they wouldn't have to stop for lunch. They ate the chicken and chips standing, then settled themselves in the two canoes, Helen and May in the first with Alice as passenger, and Pat and Fay in the second. Helen and Pat pushed their canoes away from the shore, then scrambled onto the stern and into their seats as the canoes floated free.

"Another glorious day," Helen said happily as Whitehorse disappeared behind them. She loved the outdoors more than anything, and was thrilled to have this day on the river.

"Dawson City, here we come," said Fay.

Suffused with happiness, Alice sat in the canoe as the afternoon crept slowly on. She would have preferred to paddle, but was content, too, to watch the gulls overhead and note the green shoreline of trees slip by. The canoe rocked gently each time Helen and May put their paddles in the water for a new stroke.

About five, Helen said "We're coming to Lake Laberge now, so keep to the left."

Alice looked eagerly ahead, but glanced by chance to the left. What she saw filled her with horror. There was a curl of smoke rising above the line of fir trees, a curl that seemed to get larger as she watched.

"Fire!" she shouted. "There, on the left, fire!"

Chapter 10

At Alice's cry of "Fire" all the others stopped paddling. They turned to look at the left bank where Alice was pointing.

"This is bad. No one lives along here. We'll have to alert the fire patrol," Helen exclaimed.

"How can we if no one lives here?" asked Alice timidly. Helen was so determined all of a sudden.

"Someone will have to go to the highway and phone," said Helen.

By this time the other canoe had paddled over to see what Helen thought they should do. Pat and Fay hooked their legs over the sides of both canoes so that they floated along together.

"How can we get help?" Pat asked Helen urgently.

"Well, there's a path leading from this end of Lake Laberge right over there, to the highway. One of us could run along it and get a lift to the nearest phone. It's not too far."

"Who's fastest?" asked Fay. "If someone went besides Helen, would she find the way all right?"

"Or another idea is to paddle a couple of miles further on to see if there's a phone at the cabin there," Helen continued, as if thinking aloud to herself.

"Which should we do?" May asked. By this time the current had carried them well below the fire.

"We better go to the cabin. The path would probably be quicker, but then we'd have only three paddlers to get to the cabin."

"Wait a minute, I can go," Alice broke in. "My ribs don't hurt at all except when I lift something. I can do the path and you four can do the cabin. You may have to break in if no one's home."

"You'd be fastest, too," said May. "But I've always told her never to hitchhike," she said in a worried voice, turning to Helen.

"This is an emergency," Helen stated. "If this fire gets out of control and the wind keeps blowing from the north, Whitehorse is in trouble. Let's not be silly."

May looked apologetic. "You're sure you can do it?" she asked Alice.

"Of course."

Pat and Fay released their grip on the others' canoe, then followed Helen and May as they paddled as hard as they could straight for shore.

"I thought the path was further along," Fay called back to Pat.

"It is," said Pat, "but the current is still fairly strong. We'll have to work to cut across it."

Within ten minutes they had touched shore at the end of the path. Alice leaped out of the canoe.

"Be careful, honey," May called.

"We'll wait at the cabin," Helen said. "You can come back either this way and then along the shore, or directly to the cabin. I'll walk out to the highway along the road to the cabin so you know where to go."

"I'm off," Alice said, turning on her heel and trotting away through the scattered trees.

"I hope she'll be all right," said May.

"Of course she will be," said Fay. "Don't be a nervous Nellie. Let's get going." They pushed off from shore and started to pull as hard as they could to the north.

Alice felt exhilarated to be on her own in the woods, bound on an important mission. She jogged until she was tired, walked until she again caught her breath, then trotted on. She made as much noise as she wanted, thinking that if there were a bear in the area it would be frightened away. After a while her legs began to ache, but she ignored the pain, knowing that too much was at stake to slow down. Finally, when she was beginning to feel quite sick from her exertions, she heard the sound of a car in the distance.

"The highway at last," she gasped to herself. In one last effort she sprinted to the road, crossed it, and turned to face the traffic headed for Whitehorse.

Nothing came for several minutes, and then a Camper whizzed toward her. She put out her thumb to indicate she wanted a ride, but the vehicle rushed past her, two small children peering out at her curiously from the back window.

"This won't do," she said angrily to herself. When the next vehicle, a truck, came toward her she waved her arms wildly up and down at it.

"Stop," she shouted, "please stop."

The truck tore past too, a woman in the front seat waving sociably back at Alice.

"What'll I do?" Alice thought, imagining the fire getting larger and larger and heading toward Whitehorse. This is getting desperate.

When she saw a car and trailer approaching in the distance, she stepped right into the middle of the highway and waved her arms up and down.

If he doesn't have his wits about him, I better watch out, she thought. Still waving her arms about, she prepared to jump to the side of the road if he didn't slow down.

The driver did slow down, however. In fact, he jammed on his brakes so hard that his tires squealed as he came to a stop a short way in front of Alice.

"What in Sam Hill do you think you're doing?" the driver shouted at her through his open window. "You could get yourself killed with a stunt like that." He had been frightened by what she had done, and his fear had turned to anger.

"There's a fire down near the lake," she called to him, running forward.

"A fire," he said in surprise.

"A forest fire! Could you take me to the nearest phone?"

"A forest fire? That's bad. Hop in."

Alice jumped into the seat beside him, thinking about how this was something she was never to do, then remembering how important it was to get to a phone.

The man, who was about forty, gunned his motor and sped forward toward Whitehorse.

"A fire would be a disaster! Everything's dry as tinder right now!"

"I know," Alice answered, tensely clutching to the door handle.

"Where was it?"

"Near the left bank of the river just before it enters the lake."

"There's a north wind too," the driver said. "It could be bad."

He swirled into the drive of the first house they came to. Alice sprang from the car, ran up to the house and pounded on the door.

"Forest fire," Alice shouted. "Forest fire. We've got to phone the fire patrol."

The face of the woman who pulled open the door went almost white as she realized what Alice was saying.

"I'll dial the number and you can talk to the ranger." Her voice came out in short, frightened spurts.

When the ranger came on the line, he was all business. Where did you see the smoke? he asked. How long ago? How much smoke was there? He asked her to stay where she was for the next hour, so that he could reach her by phone. She agreed, giving him the woman's phone number.

"I guess now we have to wait," said the woman. "I'll get you some cookies."

Alice went out to explain to the man what had happened, and then he drove on to Whitehorse.

"I'm picking up my sister for dinner," he said, "or I'd drive you back to where I picked you up. Will you be all right?"

"I'll be fine, thanks," she replied.

Suddenly exhausted from the excitement, she returned gladly to the sofa and collapsed in a corner. She would be able to walk back to the lake before dark even if she did rest for an hour. She was glad that the Yukon was far enough north so that it wouldn't be getting dark until ten or so.

While Alice was running toward the highway, the four women were paddling furiously toward the cabin. They found it easily, because although it was set back in the woods, there was a small rickety dock at the water's edge to which they could tie the canoes. After they had clambered onto the dock, they ran up to the cabin door.

"Anyone home?" Helen shouted, pounding on it with her fist. There was no sign of life anywhere.

"They must have gone away. We'll have to break in. There's a telephone line to the house, so we can phone from here."

The four of them huddled together and begun pushing against the front door, at first tentatively and then more boldly. None of them had ever done anything like this before. As their pushes, in unison, became stronger, they felt the door give somewhat. When they finally managed to break into the house, it was the door that gave, splitting down the middle, rather than the lock. Helen darted over to the phone, picked it up, and began to dial the operator.

"Oh no, it's dead," she exclaimed. "We won't be able to phone after all."

Pat grabbed the receiver from her, but she too soon agreed the phone was disconnected.

"We'll just have to pray Alice got through," Helen said. She went out of the house, easing past the battered door, and peered back along the river.

The smoke was clearly visible now, pouring above the trees in a steady stream.

"If the wind changes, we could be in trouble here," she said. "We'll have to take to the canoes."

The four women stared at the smoke dolefully.

"We could walk to the highway," May said, "But the wind may change, as you say." She sounded worried.

"Alice will be okay," Helen said. "She can get out by car."

They stood uncertainly in the clearing before the house, wondering what to do. Then, in the distance, they heard the sound of planes. As they watched, two planes passed over the smoke one after the other, flying low as if to examine it closely. Then they turned and made another pass, this time each dropping a cloud of red particles.

"Hurrah," Pat shouted, "we're saved. Whitehorse is saved."

"Bravo for Alice," Helen called, jumping up and down.

The planes made several more passes over the lessening smoke, then flew back toward Whitehorse. The smoke had disappeared.

"Let's all walk to the highway and welcome the hero," suggested Helen.

"Let's," exclaimed May.

Talking happily, they strolled out toward the road, half expecting Alice to come walking down the track toward them. When they reached the highway, they sat down beside it, turning to watch each vehicle that drove toward them from Whitehorse. All of them passed without slowing down. Where was Alice? Half an hour, then an hour passed. It began to get dark. May started to cry.

"Maybe Alice has been kidnapped," she sobbed. "She must have been or she'd be here by now. What shall we do?"

Chapter 11

The four women stood by the highway in despair. It was almost dark and there was still no sign of Alice. Pat put her arm around May, who was especially upset about her daughter.

"Maybe I should hitch into town and find out what's going on," said Helen uncertainly. She hated to leave them, though, when they were so upset.

Before they could make a decision, a truck from Whitehorse drove toward them and stopped. The doors opened and Alice and a fire ranger got out.

"Oh, Alice," cried May, running over and hugging her, crying harder than ever.

Alice hugged her back, embarrassed by her tears.

"Sorry we kept her so long," said the ranger jovially. "I hope you weren't worried about her. We wanted to thank her and ask what else she knew."

"Well done Alice," said Helen, patting her arm, "you saved the day."

"They asked me to stay at the house I phoned from," said Alice to her mother. "Then they came to drive me here. I'm sorry to be so late."

"Did you see the planes?" Fay broke in to ask Alice.

"I heard them go over. They did a good job."

"They sure did."

"Well, thanks again all of you," announced the ranger. "You've done important work today. If there's nothing else I can do I better be getting back. I'll take Helen with me."

"Actually there is something you can do," said Pat suddenly. "We were so anxious to meet Alice that we walked here before putting up our tents. Now that it's dark, it'll be hard to set up camp. Could you drive down to the lake and shine your headlights on the clearing so we can do the tents and get organized?"

"We should show you the accident the door of the cabin had, too," added Helen.

"Right, good idea. Let's go." Helen climbed into the truck cabin, and the rest crowded into the back of the truck. Then they bumped along the track back to the lake. The ranger parked the truck facing the clearing so that its lights shone out toward the dark water. Then the women set up the tents and carried the food down to the dock so that it wouldn't attract bears to the campsite. Meanwhile the ranger and Helen examined the cabin.

"You sure made a mess of the door," he said to Helen.

"We all did," she answered. "Who'll fix it?"

"The fire department will send someone down. It's the least we can do."

"Did you get our call?" asked Helen.

"No one mentioned a second call," said the ranger in surprise.

"That's because the phone was disconnected," Helen laughed.

"All that destruction for nothing! Actually, the cabin hasn't been used for months, so I'm not surprised."

"Thanks for telling us," teased Helen.

When everything was sorted out for the night, the four adventurers thanked the ranger and especially Helen, who then left for Whitehorse.

"I hope the rest of the canoe trip isn't as exciting as this day," Fay said as she crawled into her tent. "I'm exhausted."

"The fire rangers are really efficient," May said sleepily as she lay beside her daughter, both bundled into their sleeping bags. "What sort of questions did they ask you?"

"They wanted to know what time we saw the smoke, and how much there was, and of course where."

"What else was the ranger interested in, after he picked you up?"

"Nothing much. He did ask if I had any idea of who might have started the fire," admitted Alice.

"And you said?"

"I said I had no idea."

"Nobody at all?"

"Well, I had to say Tim and Mike might have camped here, but they may not have too. I certainly hope they didn't," said Alice.

"So do I."

"I had to mention them. The police know when they left anyway."

"Of course they do. Don't worry about it."

"Good night, brave and swift one. I love you."

"Good night."

The next morning when they started out in their two canoes, the water on Lake Laberge was fairly rough, with white caps visible in the distance.

"At least the wind is from the south," Pat said. "It'll push us along as we paddle."

The wind did help during the morning, but after their floating lunch of crackers, cheese, and peanut butter, it became so strong that the waves it stirred up threatened to splash water into the canoes. May, who was sterning the canoe, had difficulty keeping its bow in line with the shore. Their canoe began to change directions in sharp spurts, frightening Alice. She was paddling as hard as she could in the bow, but she had no control of its movement.

"Is it okay?" she called to her mother over her shoulder.

"No problem," May replied. "We'll keep on as long as we don't ship any water. I'll stay within five minutes of shore, just in case."

Alice did not answer but paddled on, putting as much power into each stroke as possible. Soon her arms were aching, but she dared not let up. They continued to paddle relentlessly for nearly an hour, followed closely by the other canoe. The wind blew strongly from the south without pause, gusting occasionally from the south west. At about three, a large wave splashed over Alice. Immediately May decided they must go to shore.

"We'll go in," she called, both to Alice and to the other canoe.

They began to swing to the left, but when they did so they shipped water as they cut across the waves moving north.

"Edge over slowly," May called, heading for land far ahead of them. Gradually they worked their way to shore, shipping more water on the way, but not enough to worry them.

"Thank heavens we made it," Alice said as she jumped ashore with the painter to tie the canoe to a nearby shrub while they unloaded. Her legs felt numb from sitting still so long, and the muscles in her arms ached from paddling. At least her ribs didn't hurt.

"I'm glad we decided to stop," May said. "It isn't safe when the waves are so high."

"What did you mean when you said we'd stay five minutes from shore?" Alice asked.

"If a huge wind comes up suddenly, we might have only five minutes to get to shore," her mother answered.

"But there was a huge wind and it took us far longer than five minutes to get here."

"That's true," said May uncertainly. They both turned to help the other canoe unload while she thought about this. "Maybe it's so that if you dump, you can swim to shore in five minutes."

They pulled the two empty canoes high up on the stony beach where they had landed, then turned them over in case it rained. They then set up the two tents on the flattest ground they could find nearby.

"What'll we do now?" asked Alice. "It's too early for dinner." "We'll go on a hike," said May brightly. She hated the afternoon being wasted in this way, when she was anxious to reach Dawson City, but she realized that as the trip's organizer she should keep up morale. The four of them climbed high up the rock behind their beach where they had a good view of Lake Laberge, then scrambled down again.

"We'll have rice for dinner," May said, again putting on an enthusiastic air. She could hardly wait for dinner and the night to be over so they could be on their way again.

"What if the wind is blowing this hard tomorrow?" Fay asked.

"It won't blow for the entire day," May said. There was no way she could waste more time on this huge lake.

They went to bed early, the wind flapping the sides of their tents crisply as they fell asleep.

When they awoke the next morning, the first thing May and Alice heard were the flappings of their tent. Far from abating overnight, the wind was stronger than ever. White caps danced all over the surface of the lake.

"Oh no," cried May in despair. "It's too windy again today. We're windblown!"

"The wind is worse than ever," Fay complained.

"Maybe it'll go down after lunch," Pat suggested.

After breakfast, they occupied themselves as well as they could for the morning. May was too upset to settle down to anything, so she stalked up and down the shoreline, glaring out at the waves to see if they might be getting smaller despite the high wind.

Fay took her backpack and set off up the hill they had climbed the previous evening. She carried the paper and pens she had bought in Whitehorse in her hand.

"May I come too?" Alice asked.

"No, I like to paint by myself," Fay answered. "I may make a sketch of the lake which I'll show you later."

Alice didn't want to join her mother, now in one of her impatient moods, so she climbed up to join Pat, who was sitting on a boulder to the far left of the tents. From there they could see May pacing about, but not hear any of the annoyed noises she was making.

"What are you doing?" Alice asked Pat.

"Thinking," Pat replied. "About women. About women and the stampede."

"Why?" asked Alice.

"Why not?" asked Pat.

They sat companionably looking across the wild surface of the lake.

"We're on the Marge of Lake Laberge," Alice said. "Remember the poem by Robert Service?"

"Of course. Isn't it wonderful?"

Pat continued to make notes about women in her notebook. Then she let Alice look through the new books she had bought in Whitehorse. Several were by women who had lived in the Yukon for years and others contained Yukon recipes for cooking.

"How would you like pickled beaver paws? Or moose tripe? Or baked gopher?" Pat laughed.

"Yuck," said Alice.

Alice picked up a thin book called *What Place is This?* by Rosalind MacPhee. "What's this about?"

"It's a book of poetry about the Yukon."

"Terrific," Alice said as she started to read it.

At lunch time the four women met for a lunch of sandwiches. May was exasperated beyond reason. "We may miss the contest in Dawson City," she exclaimed. "The waves are higher than ever and we may be windblown for days!"

Chapter 12

Had May been able to foresee the weather for the next few days, she would have been even more upset. The wind continued to blow hard for the rest of that day, and for the entire day following. After she had photographed the beach, the bushes, the rocks, and various views from the hill above their cove, she was forced to continue pacing about in frustration at the days being lost. Nor could she help but notice that Fay was entirely content to be sketching unknown subjects away from the canoes, that Pat was happily wrapped up reading and making notes on her books, and that even Alice seemed occupied on some project of her own.

"Why is nobody but me worried about the time we're wasting?" she broke out during the rice-tuna dinner of their second day of being windblown.

"You said we were coming to enjoy ourselves, and that's what we're doing," Pat answered mildly.

"This is a wonderful spot to paint," Fay enthused. "The wind on the hills is so fresh."

"Don't talk about wind," May groaned.

"I feel as if we're really getting in touch with the Yukon here," said Alice. "I've been reading some Robert Service poetry--the ballad about the marge of Lake Laberge. It's terrific. We really are on the Marge of Lake Laberge!"

"Indeed we are," May agreed sarcastically. "What if we don't reach Dawson City for Discovery Days the middle of August? That's less than two weeks away." May noted that they all frowned slightly at this idea, and was afraid she knew why.

"No panic," Pat said at last. "We can easily make up for lost time by spending longer each day in the canoes. After Lake Laberge the current goes at least four miles an hour, and sometimes as fast as nine."

"I can hardly wait," said Alice.

"We'll pray to the Great Goddess to stop the wind tomorrow," Pat said to May. "Then you can stop worrying."

The Great Goddess must have been listening with half an ear, because when they awoke the next morning the tent flies were only flapping sporadically and there were few whitecaps on the lake. May was delighted.

"Down with the tents," said May. "I'll make breakfast and we'll be off by eight."

When they began to paddle again they found they had been somewhat optimistic. The waves were as high as they had been when they were driven ashore, but now they looked at them with eyes desperate to get on with the canoe trip. Several waves splashed over Alice's bow, which should have been a signal for them to retreat to shore, but Alice pretended she did not see them and so did May. Instead they paddled their way steadily along the left shore of the lake, May keeping the canoes five minutes from land. They knew exactly what that meant.

At lunchtime they reached the old settlement of Lower Lake Laberge at the north end of the lake. From here on they would not have to paddle again if they had the patience to drift to their destination. Their jubilation at having conquered the lake was high.

"We did it!" Alice exclaimed over a cracker and cheese. "Thirty miles of really hard paddling!"

"We're terrific," Fay agreed, helping herself to the raisins.

"It takes women to do men's jobs," Pat philosophized.

"I'm back in the photography business," Pat said. "I'm going to film the Casca on the sandbar, or at least what's left of her."

"It's hard to imagine there used to be hundreds of commercial ships on the Yukon," Pat said after May had gone. She rubbed Muskol on her neck to keep away the mosquitoes that were hovering over her.

"Imagine people living right here, year after year, watching the paddlewheelers steam by," Alice said.

After lunch they paddled the thirty miles to Hootalinqua, a quick trip with the current moving them briskly along. The books they carried said this quiet area was a good one in which to see wildlife, but their only sighting was of a bald eagle at the tip of a fir tree. It glared across the river as they floated by below it, trying to pinpoint it in their cameras.

They stopped briefly to look at the few renovated log cabins which over the years had housed government officials, including police and mine inspectors, then paused to chat with two sets of canoeists who were preparing dinners over large wooden fires.

"Have you seen any moose?" Alice asked one cook, to make conversation.

"Ich spreche kein Englisch." she answered.

"Nein, no moose," the man beside her ventured carefully. They both smiled at her, shrugging their shoulders.

Alice smiled back, and turned to the other group.

"They must be German," she said, nodded toward the first group.

"Bitte?" one of the new man said.

"Germans love the Canadian north," Pat told Alice when they were out of earshot. "I've seen Yukon brochures printed in German."

They decided to visit the ship wintering yards at Hootalinqua before camping for the night. May, who had studied the maps they had with care, knew they were on the island just downstream of the former village.

"I'm not sure just where," she said, "but Pat and Fay can go down the left of the island and Alice and I will go down the right side. We can't miss them then."

"It looks like they're on the right side," Pat objected, peering at her map. "Let's all go that side. I don't want to miss anything."

"Be reasonable, Pat," May insisted. "We don't want to all miss the wintering yards. If they're not on the left side, you can come up the right side. And we'll come up the left side if they aren't on the right. There's no way anyone is going to miss anything."

"What are we hunting for anyway?" Alice asked.

"When the steamers ran on the Yukon before 1953, they had to get them out of the water in the winter so the ice wouldn't crush them," explained May. "They had wooden logs used as runners down into the water on the island, and each fall horses would pull the ships onto the island for the winter."

"Would the crew stay at Hootalinqua during the winter?" Alice persisted. She shuddered to think of spending a winter of icy cold and no daylight in a tiny log cabin.

"Maybe," her mother answered. "Or the men could get out by horse and sleigh along the Yukon Trail between Whitehorse and Dawson City. Or even by dog team along the river itself. It froze solid."

The two canoes parted company at the head of the island lying just downstream of Hootalinqua. May and Alice, who went to the right, found the wintering yards in a large clearing near the island's center. When they had turned their canoe around so that they landed bow into the current, and thus with some control, they were able to see the full extent of what had been preserved. At the back of the clearing an enormous ship, the

Evelyn, was still on blocks on the ground, never to sail again. In the bushes around her lay parts of boilers and other metal machinery, and several capstans which had been used to winch the ships ashore. Alice was intrigued with how the whole process had worked. Where had the horses done their work? Why hadn't the ships fallen over at the rough treatment they must have had? She hurried from one old remnant to another, trying to fit in the parts of the puzzle.

While Alice was studying the mechanics of the shipyard, May was photographing its contents. She used nearly an entire roll of film on the Evelyn alone; it looked so dramatic and stark rising through the green vegetation. The capstans, boilers, and paddlewheel remains also needed to be recorded in detail. May had never been happier, clicking away with her camera, the mosquitoes forming a halo around her head.

They had been in the shipyards for at least a half an hour before Alice noticed that Pat and Fay had not arrived.

"The others aren't here," she called over to her mother who was on her knees aiming her camera at the paddlewheel above her.

"They'll be along shortly," May replied in a distracted voice.

"But we've been here for ages," Alice said.

May didn't want her work disturbed. "Go and see if you can see them coming," she suggested.

Alice ran to the north end of the clearing and peered downstream, but there was no canoe to be seen. She went back to her mother.

"I can't see them anywhere," she said. "They must be lost."

"Don't be silly, dear. You couldn't get lost on the Yukon." She was studying a boiler now, deciding what surfaces she should highlight in her next shot.

"If they aren't lost, where are they?" Alice worried. "It must be getting on for an hour since we last saw them."

"Maybe they couldn't be bothered with the shipyard," May said after awhile. "Fay didn't even know it existed."

"But this is the best thing we've seen yet," Alice protested. "They'd both love it. Anybody would."

"Well, I'll just finish work here and then we'll see what's to be done." May turned to the capstan to begin documenting its reality.

Alice sat down on a log wondering if she was losing her mind. Pat and Fay had not turned up--they might be lost for the rest of the trip. Where could they be? Yet her mother was so wrapped up in her photography that she didn't seem to care. Alice couldn't hunt for their friends because she couldn't handle a canoe by herself. The more she thought, the more desperate she felt. She turned to her mother in despair.

"Mother, we have to do something. Pat and Fay are lost. This is an emergency. What shall we do?"

"Just a minute, dear. I'll be right with you," her mother said, beginning a series of wildflower shots that she had been planning for some time.

"Help!" Alice felt like shouting, but instead she sank her head in her hands in despair.

Chapter 13

When May had taken all the photographs possible, she turned brightly to Alice, who still sat with her head in her hands.

"We should go find the others," she stated. "They'll think we're the ones who are lost."

Alice rolled her eyes to heaven but didn't say anything. Together they pushed the canoe into the river, brought it alongside the shore, and carefully stepped in, Alice first.

"They're probably just below here," May said as she pushed off.

Sure enough, on the first sandbar they came to, there were Fay and Pat, their canoe pulled out of the water, sitting on two rocks side by side. They were angry.

"About time," Pat called to them as they pulled in beside the first canoe. "Why did you take so long when you knew we were waiting?"

May looked somewhat abashed, then decided to take the offensive. "Why didn't you come round to the clearing? It was terrific. There was a big ship still on shore."

"We didn't come because we couldn't make it around the end of the island. Have you any idea how strong the current is there?" demanded Fay.

"Not really," May admitted.

"Fay got hold of a branch at the end of the island," Pat said, "but when it broke it took her a while to get her paddle out again. By the time we were ready to paddle, we were too far downstream to get back."

"Is the current that strong?" Alice asked.

"You bet," said Fay. "Just you try it."

"Next time we'll decide who goes where," said Pat.

May was feeling guilty by now. "The wintering site wasn't that good," she said. "The ship there was pretty dilapidated, really."

"And the mosquitoes were awful," put in Alice.

The highlight of their next day on the river was at Little Salmon, where the Little Salmon River flowed into the Yukon. As on the other rivers, salmon were now migrating upstream to spawn after their thousand-mile swim from the Bering Sea, but they could be taken only by nets because they were no longer feeding. The Indigenous people who had their fish camp there showed Alice and the others where their cemetery was, along a path back into the woods. When the four of them followed it, they came to a group of what looked like large doll houses, each about three feet high. Each house had been built to commemorate a person who had died and been buried in the cemetery. Some had clothing or utensils which had belonged to the dead people.

"What a nice way to be remembered," Alice said in a low voice. She did not want to mar the serene atmosphere of the cemetery by speaking loudly.

"This one must be a child's," Fay said. "There's a doll you can see through the window."

"Here's a wall made of an old packing case," Pat observed.

"This one seems almost new," said Alice.

May soon began to take photographs of these dream houses as they were called, and Fay snapped some shots too.

"I can give you prints of my shots," May said, looking down her nose at Fay's cheap camera.

"I like to have my own photos," Fay smiled.

The next day they were to arrive at Carmacks, the half-way point of their trip.

"We're not supposed to stay there," Pat said. "It's supposed to be one rough town."

"What does rough mean?" Alice asked. They were floating along in a group, the canoes tied together, their occupants draped over the luggage in them, enjoying the sunshine.

"Lots of drinking, I think," answered Pat, floating her hand in the icy water, then dipping her cup into it and taking a long drink.

"And fighting afterwards, I suppose," Fay reflected.

"We have to stop there," May said. "We have to report to the police that we are still all right."

"Good," said Fay, "I want to buy some film."

"I'll buy milk and bread, while you go to the police," Pat said to May.

"I'll take a nap and watch the canoes," Alice offered. She found it difficult to sleep on the ground after the accident and was glad of extra rest.

They reached Carmacks in the afternoon, pulling in at the campsite beside one of the few bridges to cross the Yukon. When the others left to walk to the main part of town, Alice stretched out on the ground. She had just dozed off when she was startled by a loud crash, as a pick-up truck driving across the bridge hit a post at the far end. There was a commotion as by-standers helped shift the driver to a car which would drive him to a hospital, then quiet again, the only sounds the swirling of the river as it rushed past beside her and the occasional scream of a sea gull.

Fifteen minutes later there were shouts, sounds of running, and then the noise of a truck being started and driven violently, and jerkily, away. What now? Alice stood up to see. A boy passing by reported that a man had noticed that the truck which had hit the pole still had its key in the lock. He had leapt into the cabin, started the motor, and driven off toward Dawson City. A few minutes later a police cruiser crossed the bridge from town to investigate this new incident.

This is a rough town, Alice thought.

She lay down on the grass again to nap, but was roused almost immediately by the sound of heavy footsteps approaching. She looked up apprehensively, wondering nervously who it was, then burst into a smile. It was Mike followed by Tim.

"Hello there," said Mike. "We passed the rest of your group on the way into town. How goes it?"

"Terrific," said Alice. She sat up quickly not feeling tired anymore.

"I guess they told you we were windblown for two days on Lake Laberge?" Alice said.

"So were we," said Tim. "You must have been right behind us all the way down the river after that. We just got here a couple of hours ago."

"Tomorrow is the dreaded Five Finger Rapids," Alice said. She spoke as if in jest, but she had been worrying about these rapids since before the trip started.

"They're no big deal," Tim said.

"Lots of people have been drowned there," Alice objected.

"Only because they didn't know enough to take the channel at the far right," Mike said.

"There are no rocks there," Tim said. "Only lots of waves. It was dynamited clear of rubble for the steamships which used to go up and down the Yukon."

Alice and the men decided to share dinner, Alice making tinned stew, which required opening three tins, and the men supplying soup, which meant hot water poured over dry soup mix from a packet. They set out this feast on a plastic garbage bag as the three women returned from town.

"Terrific," Pat exclaimed. "We're eating in style."

"Well done," Fay said to the men.

"I got the book you wanted, on rhyming words for poets," Pat said to Alice. "Someone had left it at the general store."

As they sat around the food, Alice told the others about the excitements at the far end of the bridge. Then the conversation turned to wildlife.

"We saw a bald eagle above Hootalinqua," Alice offered.

The men laughed and looked at each other. "We saw two moose and a bear," Tim said. "Honestly."

"The moose were a mother and her calf in a slough," Mike said. "We climbed up the bank beside the marsh and were only about fifty yards away. Tim got some great shots."

"I've never had a better chance at a moose," Tim said with excitement. "In one shot I have both the moose and one of the cabins at Hootalinqua in the distance. I never dreamed I'd be so lucky."

Pat, Fay and Alice made enthusiastic noises, but May was voiceless with envy. If what he said were true, he'd be sure to win the Tourist Package competition. She tried to smile, forcing her lips into an upward curve.

"What about the bear?" Alice asked.

"He didn't see us either, at first. He came out of the bush across from our campsite last night and began to swim toward us."

"Horrors," exclaimed Alice.

"He was swept quite a way downstream so he landed way below us," Mike said. "No problem. I don't think he ever knew we were there."

"I got some terrific telephoto shots of his head," Tim said.

"That's wonderful," Fay said. May renewed her forced smile.

Before they left Carmacks to camp a few miles downstream, May approached Tim as he was packing up their food.

"The rapids should give us some good photos," she said. "I'm going to shoot the big iron rings embedded in the rock of the Five Finger Rapid channel. The paddlewheelers used to winch themselves upstream using the rings."

"I didn't know about them," said Tim.

"Most people are too afraid to even look at them as they go down the rapids," May explained.

"The rapids aren't that bad," said Tim.

"No," May agreed. "I'm looking forward to them."

The next morning began with rain. It was raining at five, when Alice first looked at her watch, again at seven, and again at eight. By that time they decided to get up anyway, even if it meant packing up wet tents.

"If we dump at the rapids it won't make any difference if our tents are wet," Alice joked.

"I thought about the rapids most of the night," Fay confessed. "The thought of them scares me silly."

"Me too," Pat said. "We'll just have to keep to the right and pray to you know who."

"I hope she's listening," said Alice.

After fastening all their gear to the thwarts with rope, so that it wouldn't be lost if they dumped in the rapids, they set off about half past nine, keeping to the right bank even though the rapids were many miles away. Usually they swept down the middle of the river where the current was strongest and paddling almost unneeded. Now they paddled through backwaters where there was almost no current at all.

As they rounded the final curve of the river, they saw the columns of rocks in the middle of the river that marked the rapids. In the left and center channels they could see angry white water thrashing about as it tumbled downward, but in the right channel there was white water too.

"We'll creep along the right bank so we aren't swept into the wrong channel," May called out.

I wish I could creep right home, Alice thought to herself.

Suddenly, about half a mile ahead of them, they saw a canoe just beginning the descent by the right channel. It was Mike and Tim, both wearing orange life jackets. Alice expected to see them hunched down on the floor of the canoe, as she intended to be, but instead Tim was sitting on the bow seat holding his camera and facing to the right. Mike was expecting to do all the paddling.

They watched as if mesmerized. They saw the canoe plough into the tossing waves, they saw Mike desperately try to keep the canoe heading forward, they saw the canoe shift suddenly to the left as it hit a large wave, and they saw Tim flung out into the crashing waves.

Chapter 14

As soon as Tim disappeared into the river, the women began to paddle as hard as they could. They forgot their fears about the rapids. Now they had to save Tim. With all their strength they paddled along the right bank, then turned to head into the far-right channel.

Alice and May went first, May steering dead center between the high channel walls. Both were kneeling on the bottom of the canoe to keep their weight low, both wore life jackets, both peered ahead, concentrating on the rushing water. They glanced up once or twice to try to spot Tim or the canoe, but neither was visible.

They hit the rough water with a shock. It punched them to the right, then to the left, while May and Alice struggled as hard as they could to keep the canoe from turning sideways to the current. They knew if they lost control, they would almost certainly dump. When they were almost through, a huge wave from the left broke into the canoe and soaked both of them, but otherwise they had mastered the rapids unharmed.

As soon as the water was smooth enough to make steering fairly easy, May joined Alice in searching for some sign of Tim or the men's canoe. There was an island ahead of them which divided the river in two, but they did not know which part to take.

"Don't paddle," Alice called back to May. "Just keep the canoe straight and we'll see which way the current takes us."

"Good thinking," May called back. She stopped paddling but kept her paddle in the water so she could turn the canoe left or right as needed to keep control.

While they waited for their route to be decided, Alice looked back to see how Pat and Fay were making out in negotiating the channel. At that moment they were in the thick of the wild water, buffeted from side to side but holding their own well. Alice saw a wave rear up and crash in over Fay, but the canoe held steady thanks to their paddling efforts. In a minute more they were safe, coasting behind Alice and May but well back from them.

By this time May realized that the current was taking her canoe to the left of the island.

"We'll go left," she called to Alice above the noise of the wave. "Go right," she turned and shouted to the canoe behind so that there would be no danger of missing the men. Pat and Fay could not hear her, but they understood what she meant by the way she waved her paddle. They began to paddle to the right while May steered toward the left.

Before they were halfway along the island, Alice spotted the men's canoe ahead of them. Mike was paddling toward a sandbar beyond the island on the right and Tim was in the water holding onto the front of the canoe.

"Tim's safe," Alice called to May.

"Thank heavens," May replied.

They paddled after the men, arriving at the sandbar at the same time. Tim crawled out of the water on his hands and knees, then collapsed on the ground. The others beached their canoes, then gathered around him.

"Let's get your wet clothes off," Mike said to Tim, helping him unzip his life jacket. Tim seemed too shocked to reply.

"We'll light a fire," said Alice, pulling dry driftwood and scrap paper from the garbage bag they kept it in.

"I'll get out dry clothes," said May, unfastening the pack that Mike indicated was Tim's.

Pat and Fay arrived only a few minutes after the others, but already everything that could be done for Tim was being done. Alice was heating water to make tea, May was rubbing Tim's feet with a towel, and Mike was opening up his sleeping bag so that it could be wrapped around him as he rested.

"Thanks for everything," Tim was saying. "I didn't think the water would be so rough."

"Were you scared when you fell in?" Alice asked.

"Shocked, mostly," Tim answered. "And cold. Five more minutes in the water and I would have been done for."

The others all gazed at him sympathetically.

"I wanted to get a shot of the iron rings. The ones in the rock that the steamers used to get up the channel," Tim explained. "I thought Mike could handle the canoe."

"I thought I could, too," said Mike ruefully.

"Did you get a shot?" Tim asked May.

They all looked at May in surprise. She had never mentioned the rings to them, nor her interest in photographing them.

"No," said May slightly embarrassed. "I realized it would be too dangerous when I saw you go over."

"It would have been suicide to take pictures from the stern," Pat said in a shocked voice.

"I guess you're right," May agreed.

"Did you suggest that Tim photograph the rings?" Pat continued.

"I did mention them to him," May said.

Tim raised his eyebrows but did not say anything. He realized now that May must have been lying when she said she would photograph the rings, but he did not want to draw attention to his gullibility.

"Are your feet warm now?" May asked.

"Yes. That's enough," Tim said to her.

They decided to have a hot lunch while they were on the sandbar since the fire was already going. Tim was not allowed to do anything while the others rallied around. Soon the canoes had all been emptied and turned over to get rid of water they had shipped in the rapids, and everyone was supplied with hot pork and beans. They ate their portions hungrily, going over again and again the events of the morning. May sat somewhat apart from the others, who were annoyed with her, and she refrained from taking any photographs that might remind them of their annoyance.

Tim was himself again, but apprehensive of the Rink Rapids which still lay ahead. He had no wish to go swimming twice in one day. The others understood his nervousness and decided to make a short day of it, camping not far below these rapids.

"They aren't bad compared to the Five Fingers," Pat assured Tim.

"In fact, if we keep to the right again it'll just be rough water. That's what my book says."

"We know about rough water," Mike said.

"Let's go in a group," Pat said. "It'll make us all feel better."

This idea appealed to all of them, so they set off in single file, first Alice and May, then Tim and Mike, and finally Fay and Pat. The Rink Rapids were as uneventful as Pat had predicted, although at first the sound of rushing water and sight of huge white waves in the distance had horrified them. However, by paddling to the far right of the river they had found the smooth channel the books had mentioned.

They camped soon after this on a large sandbar, part of an island which featured the usual spruce trees and willow bushes. It was still too early to make dinner after they had emptied the canoes, piled the food and pots near the fire, and put up their tents, so everyone had an hour's free time. Tim, who was still suffering from shock, lay down in his sleeping bag over which Mike then arranged his own. Fay set off with her pack to sketch on the far end of the island, May continued her photography of wild flowers, Mike whittled on a piece of drift wood he was fashioning into a loon, and Pat wandered along the shoreline with her notebook.

When Alice saw Pat go off alone, she ran to join her. "Can I go with you?" she asked.

"Sure," said Pat, smiling. "I'm just wandering about."

"Could you give me some advice?" Alice asked almost shyly.

"Of course, if I can," Pat answered.

"I've been thinking about poetry, and how it can convey a lot with only a few words," Alice said. "I was thinking of getting down something about the Stampeders and their feelings using poetry."

"Nothing to do with $2,000 I suppose?" Pat laughed.

Alice blushed. "Not necessarily. Well, I suppose the contest gave me the idea. Anyway, I've been working on a few rhymes with the rhyming book you got me, and some of them are about women. I wondered if you'd tell me what you thought."

"I'd love to," Pat said, delighted to hear that Alice was working on such a project.

"What about this one?" asked Alice, pulling a notebook from her pocket and reading from the first page:

> *Women were common*
> *In heels and long dresses,*
> *They marched with the strongest*
> *And cleaned up the messes.*

Alice looked at Pat hopefully. "Do you like it?"

"It has a good beat," said Pat cautiously, but "messes" sounds rather modern. Women are always cleaning up messes. Do you have another?"

Alice read another stanza:

> *Women were somehow*
> *The bravest of any*
> *They faced all the dangers*
> *A few of the many.*

"That's interesting, too," said Pat, cocking her head in thought. "Does "few" refer to women or to dangers?"

"I can't remember," laughed Alice.

"Is that all?" asked Pat.

"No, I have one last one," said Alice.

> *They came to the northwest*
> *Both women and men,*
> *They came to discover*
> *The gold there was then.*

"I think the third is best," said Pat after reflecting for awhile, "although your choice may depend on what the other verses say."

"Do you think they're worthwhile?" Alice asked anxiously. Pat hadn't been as enthusiastic as she had hoped.

Pat was looking fixedly at the ground, wondering how to answer Alice's question, when her eyes focused suddenly on the largest animal track she had ever seen, embedded in the wet sand in front of her. She was speechless, but Alice sensed her sudden intensity and looked down too.

"What'll we do," whispered Alice, aghast. "It was made by a grizzly!"

Chapter 15

Alice and Pat looked at each other in horror. If a grizzly had been here before, it might come again. Maybe it was still on the island!

"We'd better get back to the others," said Alice looking about nervously.

"What about Fay? She's at the other end of the island," said Pat. "She'll have already met it if it's still around," said Alice fatalistically.

They hurried back to the campsite, looking all around them as they went.

"There's a grizzly print along the shore," Alice called to her mother as soon as they saw her crouched beside a small yellow flower.

May stood up in alarm. "Not really!" she exclaimed.

She joined them in their rush to the campsite end of the island.

"A fresh grizzly print! Along the shore," Alice called to Tim and Mike as they reached the tents. Tim and Mike, too, sprang to their feet.

"Maybe it's only a black bear," Tim said. "They're more common."

"And less dangerous," Mike added.

"No, it was huge!" exclaimed Alice.

Everyone but Tim, who still felt weak, wanted to see the print, so they trooped back along the shore to where Alice and Pat had been talking.

"It is huge," gasped May.

"It's six inches across!" said Mike, who had been down on his hands and knees measuring it with a pocket ruler.

"Look at the size of those claws," Alice pointed out, "and how deep the print is!"

They looked around for more prints, but the bear apparently had come out of the water, stepped on the sand, and then walked over the pebbles higher up on the shore. They discussed what they should do on the way back to the campsite.

"If he's just gone through here, he probably won't come back," suggested Mike. "He's probably not still on the island or we would have heard shrieks from Fay."

"One book said you should move on if you camp near bear tracks by mistake," said May. "Bears have territories which they patrol for food of various sorts."

"Like people," Mike suggested.

"That was black bears," Alice said, ignoring Mike's attempt at humor. "Grizzlies have much larger areas to cover."

They were wondering what to do about Fay, when they saw her pushing through the willow bushes, her pack hanging from her shoulder. When they told her about the grizzly print, she was aghast.

"I might have met him," she squealed.

"Him or her," said Pat, routinely.

"What'll we do?"

They decided to take a vote about whether or not to canoe further for the night, but no one was for pushing on. It was dinner time, they were hungry, the tents were up, and they had no way of knowing if a new island would be any safer than the one they were on.

"This island isn't that big," Fay said. "I was at the other end and there's not much that would interest a bear. If he's been here recently, he probably won't come again for awhile. Or she," she added, looking defensively at Pat.

They cooked their dinner on the right side of the island a hundred yards down from the campsite, so that if any food smells remained, a bear wouldn't connect them with the tents. They all went through their packs thoroughly to make sure not even a raisin or a nut was kept by mistake in a tent. Pat, who thought they should burn the garbage to remove its smells before hanging it up, was overruled by the others who felt that burning it would advertise the presence of food on the island to all the bears in the area. She strung the plastic bag by a shoestring as high as she could reach on a spruce tree. Mike, who favored rope, managed to retie it even higher up.

They finally retired, all increasingly nervous as darkness fell.

"Remember," Mike said. "If you hear noises in the campsite, stay quiet. But if a bear actually breaks into your tent, yell for help or blow your whistle."

"We all have to go to the help of anyone actually attacked," Pat stated.

They looked at each other balefully. Each person was anxious to be helped if a bear attacked, but less anxious to rush unarmed at a bear that was attacking someone else. They wondered what they would actually do if the time came.

"As a last resort, we can pile into canoes and escape that way," Mike reminded them.

"A last resort, for sure, since we'd probably never get our gear back," Fay commented.

At first, none of them slept. They all lay still in their sleeping bags, listening intently for sounds other than the flowing water and the occasional bird. Eventually they dropped off one by one, too tired by the day's activity to worry longer about bears.

Alice awoke suddenly in the middle of the night. She heard a large animal moving about near her tent.

"Mére, it's here," she whispered, shaking May's arm. "The bear's here." May was wide awake immediately, listening intently. Sure enough, something large was pushing through the nearby willow bushes.

"Be quiet," May hissed.

They lay completely still, listening to the noises that terrified them. For ten minutes the noises continued, now closer to their tent, now closer to the other tents. Alice began to pray "Please let him go away," she begged. "Or her."

Slowly the animal began to move away from the campsite. Within a few minutes the island was quiet again, except now for rustlings in the tents.

"Did you hear that?" Mike asked Tim, but Tim had slept through it all.

"I was so scared I could hardly breathe," Fay whispered to Pat.

"I wanted to look at my watch but my hand shook so much I was afraid of making a noise," Pat said.

"I hope it's gone for good," said Fay.

Gradually they all fell asleep again, to awaken only with the daylight. When Alice climbed out of her tent to start breakfast, the campsite looked just as it had the night before. The tinned food was still piled by the evening's fire, and the garbage still hung high in the spruce tree.

"We did well by the food," she said aloud. "The bear didn't touch anything." She began to collect dry wood for the fire as the others stirred in their tents. As she put on water to boil, the canoeists emerged one by one first to wash themselves in the river, then to pack up their gear or help with the breakfast.

It was Alice, collecting more firewood near the tents, who saw a new animal track which hadn't been there the night before.

"We would have seen any tracks around here, wouldn't we?" she asked anyone who was listening. Everyone was too busy to answer her.

"Our visitor last night wasn't a bear at all," she laughed. "Look at this new print. It was a moose! "

At this remark, all of them rushed over to see what Alice had found. Sure enough, there in a sandy patch among the rocks were several large cloven- hoofed prints, just like those of deer, only larger.

Pat joined in Alice's mirth, and soon they were all laughing together.

"A moose. Why not?" chortled Fay.

"All that fear for nothing," whooped Alice.

They found by studying their maps that they could spend that night, if they were willing to paddle hard all day, at Fort Selkirk. This settlement, at the junction of the Pelly River and the Yukon, had been in existence for nearly one hundred years--first for prospectors, trappers and hunters, and then for traffic connected with the Yukon paddlewheelers.

"There wouldn't be any bears in a fort?" Alice asked hopefully.

"Of course not," May said. "There'll be a campground there and other campers."

"I'm for it," Alice said. Any place without bears was good enough for her. The men decided to stop there too. They packed up quickly and left before the others were ready so that they could be on their own for the day on the river.

The women enjoyed the day thoroughly. The sun shone hot enough so that they could sunbathe as they paddled, and they passed wildlife and "areas of historical interest" galore. On the Minto Bluffs below the campsite at Minto, where they lunched surrounded by expensive recreation vehicles and well-dressed tourists on a bus tour, they counted eleven white Dall sheep high above them, all females or young. Alice and May took turns watching them in the field glasses while their canoe circled slowly, untended, in the current. Most of the sheep were lying down, but one mother led her young from one feeding area to another, unperturbed by the steep cliffs and narrow ledges they had to negotiate. Shortly after this they saw a golden brown wolverine near the shore, and several miles beyond a porcupine on a beach drinking from the Yukon.

After the porcupine, May and Pat had an argument about which route on their maps to take. The river was wide here, and dotted with islands.

"The wider the river, the greater the current," Pat argued as the boats were linked together, their occupants enjoying a mid-afternoon snack of raisins and nuts.

"Not necessarily," May replied. "The best channels are where the paddleboats went, but they could be deep rather than wide."

"Let's test it out," said Pat when they were about ten miles from Fort Selkirk. "We'll go right where the river is wide over there, and you go left."

"Okay," said May, laughing to herself. She had noticed a number on the map which referred to "Hells Gate," a narrow section of the river but one which had been improved by the government for the paddlewheelers. Here the current ran so fast that rings had been bolted into the left bank rocks as an aid to the steamboats, just as they had been to the rocks at Five Finger Rapids. She and Alice watched the bank tear along beside them even though they weren't paddling. Pat and Fay were soon left far behind. Although May and Alice didn't paddle for the next hour, letting the current carry them along instead, it took Pat and Fay over an hour, until Slaughterhouse Slough, where cattle used to be driven and then killed for shipment to Dawson City, before they caught up. Then Pat had to laugh.

"Point taken," she said. "We got stuck on rocks twice when we went right of that island. The river was huge, but it was only about a foot deep. We had to paddle like anything to get back to where the current was, while you just flew along."

"Live and learn," said Alice smugly, glad that she had been on the winning team.

Before them, on the left, they now saw houses on the high bench before them.

"Fort Selkirk," Alice sang out. "We're here!"

Chapter 16

Until now, although they had not talked about it, the four women had all been aware of how few Yukoners they had actually spoken to about their territory. They had all sorts of information on what had happened in the past in the Yukon, on what the territory looked like, and on what plants and animals were there, but little of human interest. They were thrilled, then, when they met an old Indigenous couple at Fort Selkirk who had been born in the Yukon and lived there all their lives. They met Jake when he helped them pull up their canoes so that they rested out of the water on the steep bank.

"Better tie them down, too," he suggested. "If we have a big wind in the night the canoes could blow away."

"Good idea," Alice agreed. She tied them both to a sturdy bush growing on the bank.

"Have you lived here long?" Alice asked Jake in her friendliest manner as she lugged packs and garbage bags full of food and gear to the campsite on the flat ground high above the river.

"Twenty years," Jake offered.

"That's a long time," Alice said, looking around at the few scattered houses, many of them restorations and for show only, that made up Fort Selkirk. How could anyone stand to live in such a tiny place for twenty years?

"Hmm," replied Jake.

"Do you like it here?" she persisted, not wanting to let him escape as he seemed about to do.

"It's home," he said, shrugging his shoulders non-committally. He turned and walked toward a group of young men who were replacing some of the rotten logs in an old log house. Before he reached them, a woman came from a nearby house to talk to him.

"Do you think that's Jake's wife?" Alice asked the others.

They all turned to look at the stout, gray-haired woman dressed in trousers and a flannel shirt who stood beside him.

"Maybe," said May.

"Let's go and meet her," said Pat.

"Mightn't she be sick of nosy people?" Alice asked.

"Maybe not," May said.

"I'll go," offered Pat, thrilled at the thought of talking to a real Yukon woman.

The others saw Pat wander toward where the young men were working, watch them a moment, then turn to address Jake and the woman. As she did so, Jake shrugged and walked away but the woman stayed to talk to Pat. Soon they were immersed in conversation, their laughter at intervals reaching the others as they watched from a distance.

"Good work for Pat," May said, turning again to work on the dinner while Alice put up the tent.

"Pat can be determined," Fay laughed.

Ten minutes later, Pat returned to the others. She was delighted with herself. "They're coming for dinner!" she announced. "Daphne and Jake. Is that okay? I was sure no one would mind."

"Terrific," said May. "I wouldn't have had the nerve to ask them."

"They seemed pleased," Pat said. "At least Daphne did. Let's have the best food possible."

They emptied out their food supplies on a wooden picnic table near where they had set up the tents--there was no danger of bears here, with so many people and dogs about--then chose a gourmet meal: canned ham, boiled potatoes, carrots, and butterscotch pudding made with skim milk powder and Yukon river water. Pat set about energetically making a roaring fire, using the wood leftovers from the various carpentry reconstruction projects being carried on at the fort.

When Daphne and Jake arrived for dinner bringing their own plates, mugs and cutlery as Pat had asked them to do, the feast was spread out on the table, set off by fireweed blooms in a tin can full of water.

"This is lovely," said Daphne.

"Um," said Jake behind her.

During dinner they talked about the old days before 1952 at Fort Simpson, when paddlewheelers called regularly on their voyages between Whitehorse and Dawson City. Daphne hadn't been here then, but her parents had.

"There were two churches," she said, "an Anglican one and a Catholic one. There was a post office, a school, a stable for horses using the winter trail, and a Hudson Bay store. In the Anglican rectory over there, you can still see 1904 newspapers pasted on the wall to keep out the wind."

As soon as the meal was over, Jake drifted away from the table, but Daphne lingered over her hot chocolate with the others. She seemed delighted to have people to talk to.

"Would you mind if I took some pictures of you?" May asked her.

"Of course not," Daphne replied.

While she told them about the trap lines she and Jake used to run in winter, and about the dog teams they had before snowmobiles became popular in the early 1970s, May stalked about snapping shots of her from a number of angles, with and without the others around her. May took two pictures, then Tim joined them, too. He and Mike had set up their tent on the far side of the campground.

"May I take your picture too?" Tim asked Daphne in a pleasant manner.

"Why not?" Daphne said. May's shoulders dropped. She was annoyed at Tim for barging in on their party.

After their lazy dinner, Daphne led them through the reconstructed log cabins that dotted the site and then to the two cemeteries set far back from the water. In one were buried soldiers who had died while supervising the Goldrush so many years before. Again, Alice noted that their lives were commemorated with a short poem by Robert Service.

That night it was long past dark when they finally went to bed, and late also when they awoke the next morning. By the time they had cooked a large breakfast in celebration of the ample supply of wood for fires, the other campers had all departed. They decided once they, too, were packed up that they would paddle steadily from then on to make up for the time they had lost on Lake Laberge.

"We'll still stop for bears and moose," Alice asked the others anxiously. She didn't mind steady paddling too much now that her arms were more or less used to it, but her first priority was certainly wildlife.

"That goes without saying," May assured her.

"As long as the bear is on land and we're in canoes," Fay stated firmly. They all laughed as they prepared to leave Fort Stewart, pushing out into the Yukon River, which was slowly increasing in size as more rivers downstream emptied into it.

The women hadn't expected to see Mike and Tim again, since they had left early that morning, but the two groups continued to meet at odd intervals. That noon, when the men stopped on shore for lunch, the women passed them while sharing a floating repast. Their canoes were hooked together by Pat's and May's legs, and crackers, peanut butter and cheese passed leisurely from boat to boat and back and forth within each boat. The women waved cheerfully to the men and shouted comments at them, but the men were too far away to hear what they said. The next day, the two groups met at one of the few farmhouses they passed. Both had been lured in by the magical hand-painted sign which fronted the property and read "Fresh Home-Made Bread."

Always, each group chose small islands to make camp on, figuring that the smaller the island, the less likely a bear would be to bother with it.

On the third day after the moose/bear campsite, as it was affectionately called, the women were more tired than usual. They had paddled through steady rain all morning, and had only thoroughly dried out after several hours of afternoon sun. Their impulse had been to continue lying in the canoes the entire afternoon, basking in the sun's heat, but May had reminded them that they couldn't afford to waste time.

"We have to get to Dawson City before Discovery Days or we'll miss the contest deadline," she said.

"I'm sick of rushing," Fay countered. "This is supposed to be a holiday."

Alice felt bored by all the paddling, but she didn't say anything in case they criticized her for being weak.

"All right, let's paddle on," said Pat at last, rousing herself from the bottom of the canoe where she had been almost asleep. They reorganized themselves and paddled on.

They camped that night on the smallest island ever, perhaps thirty feet across, pleased to find a spot so unlikely to be of interest to bears.

"Any bear worth its salt will ignore us for sure," Alice stated. "We're just lucky there's enough driftwood here for fires."

"And enough flat sand for tents," Pat added.

There was no tree on which to hoist their garbage, and no chance of storing the food far from the tents, but on balance they felt less concerned with bears than usual. They fell asleep certain that they would be undisturbed all night.

Unfortunately, when it was raining on the women that morning, it had also been raining all over the Yukon Territory. Considerable rain fell on the watershed of the Yukon River and on the watersheds of the Teslin, Little

Salmon, Big Salmon, Pelly and White Rivers. During the afternoon and evening, the water of the Yukon rose noticeably. By midnight it was a foot higher than it had been the day before. As Alice turned in her sleep, her hand brushed against something wet. It was a sock, soaked with water. Unbelieving, half-asleep, she ran her hand down the side of her sleeping bag. It was wet too, sopping wet.

Chapter 17

Alice sat up in horror. She didn't know whether to waken her mother or not. If there were anything to be done, her mother would want to do it.But what could be done in the middle of the night? It was too dark to pack up their tents and belongings, too dark to paddle safely on the river.

She decided not to rouse May. She lay down to try to sleep again. When she had woken up she had not been uncomfortable with everything wet, but now that she was aware of the water she found it most distressing. When she felt for her clothes they were wet, her rhyming dictionary was wet, even the insides of her shoes were wet. She hunkered down as well as she could in her sleeping bag, thankful that at least the night wasn't cold.

Alice lay without sleeping for several hours, going over in her head what they should do when daylight came. First, they'd need to eat something, even if the wood was wet and there was no possibility of a fire. They'd have to put on wet clothes, so they'd have also to keep moving if they didn't want to catch cold. They could do that by packing up their gear, loading the canoes, and setting right off. Somehow during the day they'd have to dry their things. But what if it rained? Her thoughts went round and round while the others slept soundly on.

Gradually, as dawn approached, the tent became lighter. Alice could see first the shape of her mother, then her clothes in a puddle by her side, then the squashed black flies and mosquitoes on the tent wall above her head. When she saw her mother stir and open her eyes, she said softly,

"Don't panic, but the river rose last night and came into our tent."

"Oh no!" exclaimed May, no longer sleepy.

"Everything's wet, but we can dry them during the day."

May looked out the small window beside her head. Sure enough, water was lapping gently all around the tent.

"What about the others?" May asked.

"I don't know," said Alice. "They're still asleep."

When May looked at their tent, she saw it was still on dry ground because Pat and Fay had put it up farther from the water.

"Those lucky stiffs," said May. "I hope they'll lend us dry clothes." She held up her jeans with two fingers and watched them drip onto the tent floor.

"I had no idea the river could rise this much in one night," Alice said. "It must have poured upstream."

"Me, either," May agreed. "Everything's soaked!"

"I'll see about breakfast," Alice said. "We'll have to keep moving until we get dry if we don't want to catch cold." She unzipped the door of the tent and struggled through the small opening, making so much noise in her efforts not to get any wetter than she already was that she woke Pat and Fay. She could hear them greeting each other and the new day.

"Bad news," she called to them as she stood up. "Our tent's standing in water. The river rose during the night. All our stuff is soaked."

"That's awful," Fay called back. "Luckily we're okay."

Alice, glancing around the campsite, suddenly felt that more was wrong than just the abundance of water everywhere. When she realized what it was, she gasped.

"You're <u>not</u> okay. Your canoe's gone!" she exclaimed.

May stuck her head out of the tent, sure such bad news couldn't be true. But it was. May and Alice's canoe was still on the island, turned upside down, its painter tied to a log. The other canoe had simply disappeared.

"It's gone," May repeated. She knew Fay and Pat could never be bothered to turn it over at night, but she had assumed that they had tied it to something.

"Didn't you tie it up?" she asked Pat and Fay, who were standing in pajamas outside their tent staring at where their canoe had been.

"I can't have," admitted Fay. "We pulled it right out of the water. I never dreamed the water could rise like this."

They all looked at each other in consternation. What could they do? They were stranded on this miserable little island, even smaller than it had been the night before. Why had they been so preoccupied with bears when other dangers were at hand? There was no way one canoe could carry all four of them and their gear.

"Alice and I can go for help," suggested May. "We can reach Dawson City in two days if we paddle twelve hours a day. Then we can hire a plane to fly you out."

"A plane," Fay gasped. "That would cost a fortune!"

"What else can we do?" asked Pat.

"Two days on this island," wailed Fay. "What if the water rises some more We could drown!"

"It won't rise that much," said Pat.

"Can you lend us something dry to wear?" Alice asked Pat. She and May were beginning to shiver as the wind blew against them.

"Of course," Pat said with a start. "We were so worried about our own problems that we had no time for yours. Sorry."

Pat and Fay had only one set of dry clothes each, but they gave these to May and Alice, who quickly put them on.

"Thanks a million," May said. "I don't mind wet shoes, but wet clothes are the pits."

"These fit fine," Alice said, admiring the blue shirt and jeans Fay had lent her. "Thanks."

"Let's have breakfast before anything else," May decided. The rolled oats, sugar and bread were all soaked, but the crackers which had been lying on top of the pile of food were still edible. They sliced wet cheese to go on top of them, then ate them standing in a circle on the dry part of the island. Instead of tea, they drank water from their water bottles.

"I have another idea," Alice said suddenly. She had been feeling badly because she had lain awake for hours during the night without thinking about the canoes. If she had had more sense, she would have got up and checked them. She might have been able to rescue the other canoe before it, floated away.

"Aren't Mike and Tim behind us? We can flag them down. Surely they won't mind taking one of you in their canoe, and we can take the other."

"You're a genius," shouted Fay. "We left the bread place before they did, and we haven't seen them since. They must still be behind us."

"Unless they went around some islands and we missed them," said Pat.

"Oh." Pat's remark deflated their enthusiasm. "They may not be behind us after all," Alice conceded. "What shall we do then?"

"Let's wait a few hours," suggested May, "and if they don't come you and I will set off for Dawson City. We can leave at ten."

"Maybe I should go instead of Alice. I'm stronger and we'd make better time," suggested Pat.

"Alice is paddling well. She'll do fine," May said. Alice was grateful for her support. She didn't want to be stuck on the island when it was Pat and Fay, not she, who had neglected to tie up their canoe.

"We'll share the food, what there is of it," said Pat. "I'll do that now."

The time passed slowly. May and Alice packed up their gear, wringing each item out as well as they could, while Pat organized the food and Fay kept watch upstream for the men's canoe. At ten o'clock, they decided it was hopeless. May and Alice would have to go on. As they loaded up their canoe, Fay gave a whoop behind them.

"There they are. It's a green canoe--I'm sure it's them." A canoe was visible suddenly over a mile upstream. Quickly it came toward them as Fay, Pat and Alice waved the three paddles in wide arcs to signal it.

"Help!" Fay shouted, although there was no way the men could hear her from that distance.

Their wild activity attracted Tim and Mike, who veered from their course to approach the island.

"What's up?" Mike asked when they were within hearing range.

"We've lost a canoe," May shouted. "Can you give one of us a lift?"

When the women had explained their predicament, Tim and Mike were glad to help. They repacked their load so that there was room for Fay and her pack in the center of the canoe, while the other women loaded up their canoe with Pat in the middle.

"Are you happy to keep moving today?" asked Tim. "We want to get to Dawson City as soon as possible."

"So do we," said May, her heart sinking. She had wanted to ask Tim if his camera and photos had been lost when he dumped, but she hadn't had the nerve when she knew she was to blame for the accident. Now, it seemed that he was still planning to enter the contest. She pursed her lips in annoyance.

Alice's thoughts were more practical. "All our stuff got soaking wet when the river rose," she said. "We'll have to get our sleeping bags dry today at the very least."

"You hope," said Mike seriously. He pointed ahead to low clouds that covered the sky. Rain was already falling on the mountains to the left, and there seemed little likelihood of sunny weather ahead.

"Let's all hope," replied Alice.

They paddled in the rain steadily from ten until one, ate a floating lunch in a drizzle, and paddled again until six, when they usually looked for a place to camp. They all looked for the lost canoe, especially when they rounded a bend or passed an island but there was no sign of it. Probably it had floated into some backwater out of sight of the main river. The sky was still overcast and their gear was still wet. How could Pat and Fay have been so stupid as to leave their canoe untied? Alice thought. She might better have blamed herself and her mother for pitching their tent too near the water, but she did not do so. Soon it'll be too dark to paddle safely, she reasoned, but if we stop, mére and I won't be able to sleep, not with wet bedding in a wet tent. What on earth shall we do?

Chapter 18

As Alice was bleakly considering their prospects for the night that was fast approaching, she noticed idly that the color of the Yukon water into which she dipped her paddle every few seconds had changed from a dark to a light brown. The difference was unmistakable. She looked about to see what had caused it, and noticed a large river entering the Yukon from the left. She had long since lost their place on the map she had set out before her because the islands and twists and turns made following it so difficult, but now she realized where they must be--at the mouth of the White River. She had read that this glacier-fed river was so full of white sediment, hence its name, that it changed the color of the Yukon. Now she was looking in person at the change.

"I know where we are," she said to the others. "This must be the White River coming in from the left."

She studied the map carefully, and then gave a whoop of relief.

"And it means that Stewart River and a grocery store is not far from here. We should be there before dark."

She handed the map back so Pat could see it.

"Happy days," said May. "There's supposed to be beds for rent at Stewart River, too. We're saved."

The others, whose gear wasn't soaking wet, weren't as jubilant as Alice and May at the idea of reaching this small bit of civilization, but they were pleased at the thought of being able to stop paddling and of sleeping on a mattress rather than on the ground.

They saw the one-family settlement from a distance, and reached it after paddling madly to cross the flow of the Stewart River, which emptied into the Yukon from the right. It was already nearly dark when they fastened their canoes to the two ladders propped up against the bank of the island. They climbed these ladders carefully, letting out exclamations of surprise as they reached the top. Stewart River was a magnificent oasis in the wilderness, complete with well-kept lawn, a flower garden, a vegetable garden, and several log cabins that could be used by people travelling along the river. Without any fuss they had soon rented two cabins, one for each group, heated up on the women's stove tins of stew for dinner, and collapsed onto the beds. May had draped Alice's and her wet clothes and sleeping bags near the stove so they would dry during the night, and the couple who ran the store had kindly lent them blankets. As usual they all were exhausted, this time from worrying about the canoe and the wet gear as well as from the day's paddling, so they were asleep almost instantly.

In the morning, feeling rejuvenated, they decided to have a first-class breakfast now that they had a stove to work with. Pat chopped wood, Fay brought water from the pump, Alice tended the fire, and May cooked-- first oatmeal porridge, then scrambled eggs made with real eggs and milk bought at the store, then toast complete with kiwi fruit jelly which Pat had carted the hundreds of miles as a treat, and finally coffee. They sent Fay to ask the men to join them, but they refused the invitation. Perhaps they had had enough togetherness for the time being.

"We should make plans," May announced, as they were finishing the meal, pushing crumbs from the table to the floor where they would be swept up later.

"Yes," Pat said, shifting an empty chair so she could put her feet on it. "I'm deliciously full." It was heady to have chairs to sit on and to prop up their feet.

"What a good feed," Alice agreed.

"We are now about seventy miles from Dawson City," May continued. "We can do that in a long day of paddling, or we can take two days."

"Two days," said Fay automatically. She found continued paddling hard work and boring.

"Of course, it's not really our decision," said May. "The men have to make up their minds, and we'll have to go along with them, since they're taking Fay."

"One day," said Fay. She already knew what the men wanted and what May wanted too--to get to Dawson City as fast as possible.

"Is one day okay with everyone?" May asked, looking around.

"Might as well," Alice replied.

"I'm easy," said Pat.

"Good. Perhaps Fay could go and tell the men."

Fay started to get up from her chair, then relaxed again. "There's something else we should discuss," she said nervously. The others, startled by her tone of voice, turned to look at her.

Fay continued, "I don't have much money, and I'm worried about the lost canoe. What if we have to pay for it?"

"I thought perhaps it would be insured," May commented.

"Surely someone will find it," Alice added. "A canoe can't just disappear."

"But what if we do have to pay for it," Fay insisted. "Do we all pay equally? Or just Pat and me?" She searched their faces to see what they thought. There was a long silence, broken finally by May.

"If you hadn't left the canoe untied, we'd still have it."

There was another long pause while they stared at the wood floor or at the walls. Then Fay spoke.

"I've never canoed before. I think as leader May should have told us to make sure the canoe was always tied."

"Why am I necessarily the leader?' May asked.

"You organized the trip, and you asked Pat and me to come with you," Fay said flatly.

The atmosphere was becoming tense. Alice hated the negative vibrations that filled the room.

"Why don't we wait and see what happens?" she begged. "We'll probably find the canoe, and even if we don't, it's probably insured. After all, we paid a lot of money for it."

"Alice is right," said Pat. "Let's not panic before we have to."

Fay wasn't convinced. "I have an idea," she said "We'd all like to win the $2000 contest. Why don't we pool our efforts and use that money, if we win it, to pay for the canoe if we have to? If not, we can split the prize."

This suggestion enraged May. "What do you mean, we all want to win the money?" she demanded. "Entering the contest was my idea, and if it hadn't been for me you wouldn't even know about it."

"That's water under the bridge," said Fay. "We do know about it, and anyone can enter, so we have as much right as you to the prize."

"We'll see about that," said May angrily. "It's obvious that pictures are what they want, and I'm a professional photographer."

"So is Tim," said Fay maliciously.

May ignored her remark. "Why would I agree to join forces with you? What can any of you do that could be used for the contest?"

Even Alice was annoyed by her mother's remark. After all, she could write poetry, Pat had gathered together a lot of material about women, and Fay was a good artist.

Fay pushed back her chair roughly, stood up and marched from the room. Pat and Alice began clearing away the dirty plates noisily. All the pleasure generated by breakfast was gone.

May was embarrassed by their obvious anger.

"I didn't mean to be rude," she said, "but we might as well face facts."

"Let's face packing everything up," Pat snapped.

The men were more than keen to reach Dawson City that night, so they set off in the two canoes just before nine. Again they paddled steadily all morning, this time over water so discoloured that they stopped at a creek to fill up their water containers rather than drink from the river.   Pat and Fay, as passengers, spent their time studying the low and high banks and mountains they passed with binoculars for signs of wildlife. They were rewarded with a black bear, so high up and far away on a mountain slope that they would have mistaken it for a rock if it had not been moving, and with a peregrine falcon which screamed at them from a cliff a hundred feet above their heads.

For lunch, May suggested that they join the canoes together and float awhile as they passed around bread and sardines and cheese, but the others said they would make better time on their own. No one felt disposed to be friendly. Pat and Fay took charge of half of the food and dispensed it within their own canoes.

The excitement of seeing a wild peregrine falcon, was to be of crucial importance to the group. Whereas earlier they had stayed in the center of the river where the current was fastest, now they began to make forays nearer to the shore so they could look for peregrines there; the current was fairly fast at the base of the cliffs on which peregrines roosted so they did not waste much time. Both canoes had swung wide to the left above what they later thought was Galena Creek, planning to pass close under the cliffs beyond the creek, which meant they passed close to the creek mouth. As they did so, they noticed a make-shift dock beside the creek to which was tied a green canoe identical to the one they had lost.

"Let's land," Fay shouted, so that both the men and the other canoe behind her heard. "I think that's our canoe!"

Chapter 19

Because of the current the two canoes pulled to shore somewhat beyond the dock, but in no time their occupants had hauled them out of the water and run back to the tied-up canoe.

"It looks the same, but how can we be sure?" May asked Fay. "There must be dozens of green canoes on the river."

"It's ours, it really is," Fay broke in. "Look," she said, pointing to a piece of tartan cloth tied to the front gunwhal, "I was using that as a towel when it rained!"

Sure enough, there was the piece of cloth, torn from an old shirt, that the women had all seen before.

"The three paddles and life jackets are here too," Alice said happily. "We're saved--financially, anyway."

As they stood about admiring the boat, a man came toward them from a large house set well back from the river.

"Howdy," he said.

"This is our canoe," Pat said bluntly, wondering what they would do if the man denied it. "It broke away from our campsite two days ago when the river rose."

"I thought it must be something like that. Two Germans stopped in with it early this morning. They found it floating down the river and didn't know what to do with it. They were gonna tow it to Dawson, but found it too much bother."

"They were wonderful," May said.

"I was gonna take it my next trip to Dawson," the man said, "but now you've saved me the trouble."

"What were their names?" Pat asked. "We'll have to find them and thank them."

"I don't know," the man said. "I didn't ask." He invited the canoeists up for coffee, but they decided to head on to Dawson City, now that they were so close.

Pat and Fay ferried the canoe down to the place where the others were pulled out, then loaded it with their gear from these two canoes. Within ten minutes, the reorganization was complete, but Pat took extra time to rearrange their packs and food so that the men could leave before the rest of them.

"Tim and Mike must have been getting rather sick of us," she said after they had thanked the men profusely for helping them out and waved them on their way.

"I must say I feel badly that I didn't appreciate them before," May admitted.

They set off together shortly after, cheered even more by the scream of another peregrine falcon on the cliffs beyond the creek.

"This really is our lucky day," said Alice, peering at the bird with the field glasses while her mother kept the canoe on course.

As they neared Dawson City, their final day on the river began to seem not exactly unlucky, but sad. They had covered thirty-five miles on foot, four hundred and sixty miles by canoe, and now their adventures were nearly over. No more lumpy beds, no more mosquitoes, no more soakings from the rain, but also no more wonder each day as bends in the swift-flowing river revealed endless new vistas of cliffs, mountains, sunlight skies, and wild animals.

The sun was low in the sky when they caught their first glimpse of the open scar which marked the hill under which Dawson City nestled. From then on they kept to the right shore so that they wouldn't miss their destination. When they came around the last bend and saw the cluster of buildings making up this historic settlement ahead of them, Alice had a lump in her throat. Good-bye to adventure, good-bye to our mighty river, she thought. We're here at last.

They floated slowly past most of the town, then stopped behind an airplane at what seemed to be a public dock. While May went up to report their arrival to the representative of their canoe rental firm, the others unloaded their gear onto the dock, pulled up the canoes, then lugged them up the bank to join a pile of canoes brought in earlier. Alice then carried the paddles and the lifejackets to the woman May was talking to in a nearby wooden tourist building.

"Have a good trip, did you?" the woman asked Alice routinely, standing the six paddles in a corner of the room.

"Wonderful. "

"No trouble with the canoes?"

Alice and May exchanged glances. "Nothing to worry about," replied May.

"Good. Here 's your receipt. Enjoy Discovery Days." She herself was anxious to close up so that she could begin celebrations.

"Do you know when the entries to the Tourist Package competition have to be in?" May asked her as she was ushering them out the door.

"Saturday at noon," she replied. She might not have known except that her boyfriend was in charge of the contest.

"And this is Thursday?" May asked, just to be sure. It was hard to keep track of the days when one was on the river.

"Yes," the woman laughed, locking the door.

From the dock, they put on their backpacks, divided the bags of food and pots among them, and marched away from the river with all their belongings to find places to sleep. May and Alice were fortunate to discover a motel with a vacancy--it was fully booked for the rest of the Discovery Days weekend--where they could finish drying out their clothes and sleeping bags. Pat and Fay found a place for their tent at a commercial campground where Alice and May could join them the following day.

"Tomorrow I'll have to get my prints developed," May said to Alice sleepily before they dozed off. "And arrange my entry. I haven't got much time."

Her remarks made Alice feel better. This might be the end of their trip, but the excitement of the contest was still ahead.

Friday was a busy day for everyone in Dawson City. Organizers were hanging up banners, arranging for the tug of war, and cleaning the streets and swimming pool, while the canoeists were either sight-seeing, or preparing their entries for the Tourist Package contest, or both. When May went to the drug store to hand in her films, she met Tim there also arranging to have his films processed during the day. When she hurried with Alice up the hill at the back of the town to hear and photograph an actor reciting poetry by Robert Service in front of Service's renovated cabin, with grass growing on its roof, there was Tim again, this time with Mike.

"Is he following us?" May whispered to Alice as they settled themselves on a backless wooden bench.

"They're only two poetry readings a day," Alice whispered back. "I'm surprised Pat and Fay aren't here, too."

"They probably slept in " May murmured.

Far from sleeping in, Pat and Fay had been up for hours, Pat touring early buildings, the paddlewheeler Keno, and the museum to get inspiration for her entry. Fay visited the cemetery above the town where it was quiet and she could sketch. Both knew that they had just one day to prepare for the competition.

Pat, by chance, met Alice and May at noon outside a restaurant, so they had lunch together before going their separate ways in the afternoon. Alice was planning to hear readings from the work of Jack London, whose cabin had been moved from upriver to Dawson City, May was going on a guided tour of the town core after picking up her Chilkoot slides at the post office, and Pat was looking forward to an illustrated talk on the Yukon given in the Palace Grand Theatre. It was in this building, reconstructed by the government to look just as it had in 1900, that the Tourist Package entrants would be on display on Saturday afternoon. They would be judged on Sunday at noon, then cleared away on Monday.

By Saturday evening, the two tents in the commercial campground were bustling with activity. Alice had cleared out of their tent so that May could spread all her pictures about her before choosing which ones to mount on the large sheets of blue cardboard she had bought. In a second exhibit she had the slides of the Chilkoot Trail which she hoped the organizers would let her show during the judging. Alice herself sat by the door of the tent copying verses in as decorative a hand as she could on sheets of expensive white paper also purchased at the bookstore.

Fay was in the other tent arranging her entry, which consisted entirely of sketches. These she was pinning to large yellow cardboard sheets, printing information about each in neat lettering below. Pat, like Alice, was sitting outside her tent with a scrap of paper on which she was planning an arrangement of information about Yukon women. She was frowning to herself, unable to decide exactly how she should proceed.

"Can I bother you for a minute?" Alice asked Pat in a low voice. She didn't want to disturb the others.

"Sure," said Pat looking up.

"What do you think of this?" She spread out a page on her lap and began to read:

Men came to the Klondike
But women came too,

They came for adventure
Or for something to do.

"Oh Alice," Pat laughed so hard tears ran down her cheeks. "You really are something. That's every bit as good as the others. You're wonderful."

Alice put the poem away uncertainly. Was Pat pulling her leg?

Chapter 20

Twenty contestants spent Saturday morning arranging their entries on the stage of the Palace Grand Theatre so that they would be ready by noon. Alice was amazed at the variety of the offerings. Her sheaf of verses depicting the history of the Klondike Gold Rush had to share a table not only with Pat's entry, called "Women Love the Yukon Too" and featuring charts of information on women as well as four women's books, but also with a pile of old rusty tin cans and implements piled there by two ten-year-old boys.

"You aren't allowed to collect old artifacts like that from the Stampede, are you?" Alice said to one of them.

"Oh, these aren't old," he answered. "We found them in the dump and thought they'd make people think of the real thing."

"That's true," said Alice doubtfully. She wished her poems could be somewhere else.

May had somehow grabbed a table all for herself and was setting out her displays of cardboard and a tray of slides. The judges wouldn't arrange for the slides to be shown while the exhibits were open to the public, but had assured her that they would look at them in private during the judging.

Near May were two women trying to arrange a quilt they had made over a screen so that it was draped artistically but still allowed the tiny stitches they had invested in the winding blue ribbon of the Yukon River to be admired. Beyond them was Tim's display of photographs set off by the loon Mike had fashioned out of driftwood. May and Alice both wandered over to this display to study his photographs. May was put out to see that his shot of a moose against the background of Hootalinqua had turned out very well. She had hoped that his camera or film might have got wet when he fell out of his canoe. The photograph below the moose was even more annoying; there was the iron ring, bolted into the cliff at the Five Finger Rapids, the very picture she had pretended she wanted. Tim must have taken the shot, then dropped his camera into the canoe before he fell overboard. She walked back in a huff to her own table when she saw Tim and Mike walking toward their display. Alice was left to be polite.

"Your pictures are really good," she said to Tim. "That moose is terrific."

"Thanks. Did your mom like it too?" he laughed.

"Very much," Alice lied. She felt it diplomatic not to mention the iron ring.

"Your loon worked out beautifully, Mike," she said.

Mike bowed slightly in thanks. "There certainly is variety here," he observed, looking around the stage.

When she left the men, Alice sauntered over to the other side of the stage, her eye caught by a table with a broken violin on it beside which rested a music score. This was a song, "The North West is Free," with lyrics on the wonders of the land where the Stampeders did stand.

"That fiddle came from the dump too," the young lad who shared Alice's table came over and said to her.

"I guess you're sorry you didn't take it," Alice teased.

"Yea," he answered solemnly.

Fay's display was at the far edge of the stage. Alice examined her drawings with interest, the first time she had been allowed to see them. They were beautifully done, one of the view over Lake Laberge, one of a fireweed bloom, but most dramatically one of the red shoes. Alice studied it carefully, noting the detail of the bows and of the heels and the way the shadows fell. She remembered that Fay had taken a picture of the shoes, but she was certain that Fay had not had any film developed in Whitehorse. There was no doubt about it. Fay could not have depicted the shoes in such detail, exactly the way Alice remembered them, without having taken them with her. It was Fay who had stolen the shoes.

All Saturday afternoon, while the celebrating crowds surged up and down the streets of Dawson City, Alice worried about the shoes. What should she do? She was the only one who knew they had been stolen. If she told the police, Fay would be fined and she had so little money. The police might even tell her how they had found out about the shoes. If she told May or Pat, it would destroy the harmony of their group. But if she didn't tell the police, the shoes would probably leave the Yukon and lose their historic value. Or they might end up in the boy's fruitful Dawson City dump.

In the evening, when the entire population of Dawson City seemed to be squeezed into Diamond Tooth Gertie's Gambling Hall, Alice met Mike, who was also wandering about watching people play Black Jack. As soon as she saw him alone, she knew what she would do.

"May I share a problem with you?" she asked.

"Of course," he answered, puzzled at her serious manner.

"You know the red shoes you showed me from the Chilkoot? Fay stole them. That's how she was able to draw them so well for her picture in the contest."

Mike's jaw dropped open. "You're kidding," he exclaimed.

"No," Alice assured him. "When I went by the boulder they were hidden under the morning after we looked at them, they were gone. I thought maybe you and Tim had them."

Mike looked shocked. "It's against the law to take artifacts like that," he said. "You'll have to tell the police."

Before she could answer, Pat had joined them and was pulling Alice toward the stage show.

"They're having the can-can dancers soon," she laughed. "We have to be in the front row so we can hiss." By the time Alice could break free without hurting Pat's feelings, Mike was lost in the crowd.

That night before she went to sleep, and during Sunday morning, Alice still couldn't make up her mind what to do. She had a headache from worry. As she was walking with the others at noon to the Palace Grand Theatre to hear who had won, she saw Tim on the board sidewalk talking to a policeman. Without further thought, she went over to join them, as if impelled by fate. Tim must be telling the policeman about the shoes, so she would show that she, too, had integrity. She didn't have time to be nervous.

"We camped about eight miles along Lake Laberge on our first night out," Tim was saying to the policeman. "And we have a witness. A fisherman came over to our campsite in the morning and sold us a pound of salmon."

"We're just checking," said the policeman apologetically, turning away.

"He wondered if we could have started a fire outside Whitehorse the day after we left there," Tim explained to Alice. "He got my name from the Whitehorse police."

"I knew about the fire," Alice said weakly. Her resolve to discuss the shoes with the police had completely evaporated at this unexpected topic of the fire. She now felt relieved that the police hadn't mentioned her connection with the fire and that she had given Mike's and Tim's names to the authorities. Her mind was in a turmoil as they entered the theatre and sat down in the orchestra seats. The master of ceremonies was already announcing the contest winners.

"We had a more varied selection of entries to choose from than we had anticipated," he was saying, waving his hand to include the loon, the rusty cans and the broken fiddle," but because of this we have decided to divide up the prize money." The audience shifted nervously, full of anticipation.

"Five hundred dollars goes to the person who wrote the music and lyrics to "The North West is Free." He held up the music and the broken violin while everyone clapped loudly except May, who lightly slapped her leg with the fingers of her left hand.

"Five hundred dollars goes to these slides of climbing the Chilkoot Trail," he announced, holding up May's slides while May's face alternated between looking pleased at having won, but sad at not having won more. There was more clapping.

"Five hundred dollars goes to this magnificent photograph of a moose near Hootalinqua," he said, pointing to Tim's picture, "and five hundred dollars goes to this verse which we intend to use in our advertising next year." He opened Alice' s collection of poetry and read:

> *Gold's where you find it*
> *Wherever you go,*
> *On the Chilkoot's steep splendor*
> *Or the Yukon's broad flow.*

Everyone clapped again, this time May as hard as anyone, while Alice blushed. The audience was getting up to examine the winning entries when the master of ceremonies called for them to be seated again for a final announcement.

"It is my sad duty to report that one contestant has been guilty of removing an artifact from the Chilkoot Trail in her eagerness to win the prize." Alice caught Mike's eye at this point and saw him shrug. He must have told the police as she should have done!

"We have reported this matter to the police. The artifact will be taken from her and returned to the Chilkoot ranger, and she will be fined. Our heritage depends upon respect for the past from all of us."

He paused for a moment to let this sentiment sink in. "Congratulations to our winners," he finished. "Will they please come up, give us written permission to use their material, and collect their cheques."

The room erupted in excited talk as the announcer finished speaking. Alice and May hugged each other, Pat hugged them both, then all of them including Mike congratulated Tim. Only Fay was left out; she had slipped away to wrap up the red shoes for their journey back to the Chilkoot.